TYLER'S
MOUNTAIN MAGIC

BY

MALCOLM ATER

TYLER'S MOUNTAIN MAGIC

For information Call: 304-876-6985
or email: player3519@hotmail.com

This novel is a work of fiction about the Harpers Ferry
Junior High wrestling team. Names, characters, places
and incidents are products of the author's imagination
or are used fictitiously. Any resemblance to actual
events or locales or persons, living or dead, is entirely
coincidental.

ISBN: 0615440819
EAN-13: 978-0615440811

LCCN: 2011901476

BLUE RIDGE MOUNTAIN BOOKS, LLC
P.O. Box 704
Shepherdstown, WV 25443
(304) 876-6985
email: BlueRidgeMountainBooks@hotmail.com
Web site: BlueRidgeMountainBooks.com

(Additional books may be purchased at Amazon.com,
BlueRidgeMountainBooks.com, and other fine book outlets.)

Printed in the United States of America

Dedicated to
TYLER MOORE
A teenage boy with more guts and courage than
anyone I've ever known.

What other writers say about Tyler's Mountain Magic...

"Tyler's Mountain Magic has great moral fabric besides
the central story that follows the dreams of a teenage
boy. I laughed. I cried. If anyone can read this book
without crying, they don't have a heart."
Bob O'Connor, author of six historical fiction novels

"Malcolm Ater takes the reader inside the world of a
special boy who, through his faith, single-handedly
inspires his friends, his school, his community, and
everyone he touches. A must read."
Lauren Carr, author of four murder mysteries

A portion of the proceeds from the sale of this book
will go the Cystic Fibrosis Foundation for research
in Tyler Moore's name.

Prologue

S ome things are made to happen. Other things can't be explained. It was like a curse seemed to hang over our town of Harpers Ferry and the surrounding Blue Ridge Mountain where most of us lived. Nothing good seemed to come our way, especially at our little junior high school. We were used to being kicked around. If something good was going to happen, Harpers Ferry was the last place you'd expect to find it. That's what everyone thought. Except Tyler. He always believed something magical would happen to us if we only believed in ourselves.

No one knew why Tyler had his illness. Anyone else would have been bitter, but not Tyler. He learned to live with it and never complained, and most of us just accepted that he often got sick. No matter how many times he went to the hospital, we always expected him to come back home to the mountain. All Tyler wanted out of life was to be normal, to be accepted as a regular kid. But he often told me that he wanted to be a part of something special, something that had never been done before. Maybe that's what drove him. Maybe that's why things happened as they did.

When we were in the seventh grade, a bunch of us went out for our junior high wrestling team. No one expected us to do well. It was just something to do since we all liked sports, even if we never won. At our school we never won at anything. We had a losing team in every sport since the old high school became a junior high, and that was twenty-five years ago. Not one winning season in anything. Worse, we had never beaten our cross-county rival, Mecklenburg Junior High, a single time in any sport. Not once. We were always fighting them and we always lost. So you could say we were pretty well-conditioned to losing. Some people said the curse on Harpers Ferry came from John Brown back in 1859 when he was captured and hanged trying to take over our town arsenal. I just thought God had forgotten about us.

Tyler was the only one who believed in our team. It was funny, because Tyler wasn't a very good wrestler, at least not in the beginning. His first year at Harpers Ferry he stunk, but so did a lot of other boys, me included. But he kept saying that if we all stuck together, if we didn't give up, something good was going to happen to our team. So for three years we all stuck together.

Nobody could have been prepared for what happened to us during our last year at Harpers Ferry. It was good, it was bad, and it was ugly. But it was Tyler's dream. Maybe if you want something bad enough, good things really will happen to you. That's what Tyler always said. But everyone knew that nothing came free and easy at Harpers Ferry.

Tyler's dream would eventually take us on the most magical sports ride in West Virginia history. But this story isn't really about our team. It's about a boy named Tyler who used his mountain magic to end a war that had been going on in our county forever. It's about a teammate who taught us the meaning of friendship and courage and holding on to the important things in life. Unfortunately, everything comes with a price.

You won't see any signs in our town honoring John Brown and his infamous raid that ignited the Civil War. But you will see a sign at the entrance to Harpers Ferry that honors a boy named Tyler Moore who brought his dream to our small town. Call it *Tyler's Mountain Magic.*

Part One
Seventh Grade

1

Tyler Moore hurried out of his seventh grade English class, his head down as he rumbled through the hallway. Mrs. Jarvis had given him another D on his last paper and he wasn't happy about it. His mother would have a fit. Why couldn't you just write the way you talked? Why did teachers have to complicate everything? He grudgingly thought how complicated his own life had always been.

Nothing had ever been easy for him. Not good grades, not athletics, not anything. He wanted so much to be successful at something, anything, to make a name for himself, but the only thing he was good at was continually being sick and getting rushed to the hospital. All he wanted was the opportunity to be *someone*. But he knew he had as much chance of standing out at something as he did of living a normal life, or even living into his twenties, for that matter.

He rushed around the corner, his head still down, the injustice of his grade and his whole life screaming in his brain. He never saw the figure approaching from the opposite direction.

"Hey!" someone called out a moment before he slammed into the figure, his books falling to the floor. Tyler knelt down to pick up his books, then looked up at the man looming over him.

He recognized him as Coach Mac Waters, the school's wrestling coach.

"You need to watch where you're going," the coach said.

"Sorry," mumbled Tyler, standing up. "I was in a hurry to get to the cafeteria."

"I just had lunch there," said the coach, rolling his eyes. "It's nothing to rush for, believe me."

Tyler smiled at the coach. It didn't look like he was going to get lunch detention.

Coach Waters gave Tyler an appraising look and nodded. "Son, how would you like to be a champion? We could use your energy on the wrestling mats."

No one had ever asked Tyler if he wanted to be a champion. And he certainly didn't *look* like a champion. He barely weighed 85 pounds and looked pale and weak with thin arms that stuck out from his body like sticks.

Tyler had cystic fibrosis. He frequently had breathing problems that congested his lungs with thick mucus and landed him in the hospital, sometimes for days or even a week at a time. But he did like sports and he *was* competitive. No one could take that away from him. He always said that he just wanted to be *normal,* and that meant playing sports like anyone else.

The coach scrutinized him again. "I think you'll do fine. Come out for the team."

"I've wrestled for two years in the youth league," Tyler told him proudly. He didn't mention that he had never won a match.

The coach looked at him with more interest. "Really?" He had to smile at the way Tyler puffed out his chest. "What's your name, son?"

"Tyler Moore," he answered importantly, not knowing that Coach Waters told every boy he could be a champion, even skinny ones like Tyler.

This was the fifth year that Harpers Ferry Junior High School had a wrestling team. It had been started at the insistence of the school's alumni association. They argued that if the only other junior high in the county, Mecklenburg Junior High, was allowed to have a team, Harpers Ferry should have one, too. The appointment of Mac Waters as wrestling coach had not been a popular choice in other parts of the county.

Several other men had wanted the job, and still did. They were the youth league coaches, most of whom lived in the Mecklenburg school district. But the principal at Harpers Ferry had insisted they hire "one of its own." Mac Waters had gotten the job only because he actually taught at the school. And while Mecklenburg had long ago established itself as a state wrestling power, the early wrestling teams at Harpers Ferry struggled through losing seasons like every other sport at the school. Mac Waters' coaching ability was constantly being criticized by the youth league coaches, and many of them wanted him to fail.

"You look like you have the makings of a winner, Tyler, and one day you'll walk these halls as a champion," said Coach Waters to the wide-eyed seventh grader. "Practice starts a week from Monday, so be sure you get a physical before then. See you at practice." He was gone before Tyler could answer.

He said I could be a champion, Tyler repeated to himself, his back straighter and his head up as he continued towards the cafeteria. He turned down the main hallway and saw Danny Schneider, Travis Nutter and me hurrying up the stairs from the gym.

"Hey! Guess what?" Tyler said excitedly. "Coach Waters just asked me to come out for the wrestling team. He said I could be a champion!"

"That's exactly what he said to me this morning!" beamed Travis, nodding his head.

"Me, too," I chimed in.

Danny rolled his eyes at Tyler. "You weren't exactly a champion in that silly youth league." Danny was shorter than Tyler and had more of a wrestler's build, but he didn't care for the sport. He and Tyler lived fifty yards away from each other on Blue Ridge Mountain and had been best friends forever. Danny was always going to visit him in the hospital. Some of the stories he told were enough to make even a healthy kid sick. Like the nurses putting tubes down Tyler's throat to drain the mucus from his lungs. Sticking tubes in his skinny little arms to feed him intravenously, sick stuff like that. Best friends or not, it wasn't an easy thing to watch. Of course, *Tyler had to go through it,* not just watch it.

Tyler winked over at me and Travis. "You know, guys, we could be the start of something big here. We might even be able to win a few trophies, unlike the football or basketball teams," he said with exaggeration, eyeing Danny.

"Hey, we did win two games in football this year. That's better than we usually do," said Danny defensively, a reserve running back on the team.

"Yeah, but a winless season is never out of the question at Harpers Ferry," suggested Tyler, and Travis and I laughed.

"You guys are just sore because I'm going out for the basketball team instead of wrestling," countered Danny.

"How many games did they win in basketball last year? Three?" asked Tyler.

"It's not our fault, anyhow," offered Danny. "It's the curse of John Brown." At this we all nodded as we continued down the hallway.

2

Tyler finished the mixed peas and carrots on his plate before bringing up wrestling. His mother was always harping how important it was to eat all his vegetables. The conversation would be sticky enough without upsetting her if he didn't eat everything. "Coach Waters stopped me in the hallway today," he began pleasantly, looking across the table at his father. "He asked me to come out for the wrestling team. He said I could be a champion one day."

"He did?" said Mr. Moore with a smile. "I bet you could, too."

The fork that Tyler's mother was holding dropped loudly against her plate. "I thought we had already been through this. We made a decision." She glared at her husband.

Tyler had expected this. "All my friends except Danny are going out for the team, and everyone says it's a lot of fun. The coaches are really nice," he said hopefully, his eyes pleading with his father. Tyler idolized his father, a huge bear of a man that people affectionately called Big Bill. He had been a standout-wrestling champion in high school and college, but had never tried to press his son into wrestling. He just wanted Tyler to have fun and enjoy every minute of his life.

"You were always watching your weight in the youth league. I'm not going to stand for that anymore," said his mother.

"Besides, you never even won a match," she added, bringing a frown to Tyler's face.

"All the more reason we should let the boy wrestle," his father said heartily, reaching over to rub Tyler by the shoulder. "It'll happen one day."

"Bill, I don't want Tyler wrestling," said his mother firmly. "He needs to gain as much weight as possible, not try to lose it. It's too dangerous in his condition."

"Will you stop acting like I'm going to die tomorrow!" said Tyler, his voice rising. "I'm thirteen and can make my own decisions. It's my life, and this is what I want to do. I want to do things that other kids do. Don't you see, Mom? All I want to be is a *normal kid!*"

"Oh, Tyler, I *do* want you to be a normal boy," she said, beginning to sob. "But your last attack in August almost killed you!"

Tyler drew in a deep breath. "Mom, I know the facts," he said, more like a young man than a young teenager. "I can't control what's going to happen, but I *do* want to control how I live my life. And right now I want to go out for the wrestling team and be with my friends. I want to have fun. I want to forget that I'm different from everyone else. Is that too much to ask?" He rose from the table and went over to put his arm around his mother.

Mrs. Moore was fully sobbing now. "I just want what's best for you. Why can't you go out for something like basketball?"

"I'm too small for basketball." He grinned at his father. "Besides, Dad says basketball is a sissy sport. Wrestling is for men. If I don't grow up to be a man, at least I can be one when I wrestle." He was trying to make a joke, but it only brought more tears to his mother.

"Wrestling takes too much out of you. You'll cut down on what you eat and try to control your weight." She knew what would happen. "You're going to start growing. The doctor said you need all the weight you can gain."

Tyler looked for help from his father. "Dad? This is something I want to do."

Mr. Moore studied his wife. She was only trying to protect Tyler, but sometimes she smothered him. The boy needed to live his own life. "I want to enjoy every moment I have with my family, and that means giving each other encouragement," he told her. "We can't shelter Tyler forever. There are some things that he's old enough to decide for himself, and this is one of them." Bill Moore looked at Tyler proudly. Illness or not, the boy was everything he wanted in a son.

"Not the wrestling!" repeated his mother again. "It will take too much out of him!"

Tyler's father nodded over his shoulder. "Why don't you go to your room and get your homework done? Your mother and I need to talk," he said.

Tyler nodded glumly. He knew this would happen. His mother was almost shouting, *"He's my only child! I don't want to lose him!"*

As Tyler trudged up the stairs, his father replied, *"And he's my only child, too. But I also want him to be happy. Let him enjoy his life while he still can."*

3

The view from Harpers Ferry is one of America's greatest natural treasures. Thomas Jefferson wrote to a friend in Europe that the sight of the Blue Ridge Mountain and the point where the Potomac and Shenandoah Rivers meet at Harpers Ferry *"was well worth a trip across the Atlantic to see."* But in 1997, the Blue Ridge Mountain was filled with dreary trailers and mobile homes that people lived in. More than a few yards were littered with broken-down cars or heaps of junk lining the porches. During the winter, many kids would go to school wearing only a T-shirt and thin jacket to keep warm. And although indoor plumbing had finally come to our part of the county twenty years earlier, the numerous out-houses in the backyards were a constant reminder that the past wasn't too far away.

The students who went to Harpers Ferry were different from the students on the other side of the county at Mecklenburg Junior High. We were poor, plain and simple.

"I can't wait to start throwing people around on the wrestling mat," Tyler said brazenly as he ate lunch in the cafeteria with Danny, Travis and me. His mother had finally relented and given him permission to wrestle but had not been happy about it. His father just wanted him to have fun, whether he won any matches or not. "You oughta come out to our first practice today, Danny, just to see what it's like."

"Basketball tryouts start today," Danny reminded him. "Besides, I already know what wrestling is like. I'm not about to go prancing around in tights trying to get on top of another guy."

At this the rest of us giggled. Wearing a wrestler's uniform, or singlet as it was called, had always been a bone of contention with Danny. "I think Danny's afraid that some girls will see the outline of his manhood through his singlet," suggested Travis wryly.

"Or not see anything at all," howled Tyler, laughing so hard that the other students around us turned with questioning stares to see what was so funny.

"I heard there were going to be a lot of starting positions open on the wrestling team," Tyler said after we put our lunch trays away and headed to fifth period class. "A lot of ninth graders started last year and some other guys moved away. Coach Waters said the seventh graders will have a real chance to contribute this year."

"Sounds like he's already making excuses," scoffed Danny.

"Look, the football and basketball teams have never beaten Mecklenburg and probably never will. But one day we'll beat them in wrestling," said Tyler, fired up about wrestling ever since Coach Waters asked him to come out for the team. "I want to be a part of something really big here at Harpers Ferry. I want to be part of something that's never been done before."

"You don't get it, Tyler," Danny said in a discouraged tone. "When it comes to sports, Harpers Ferry has always been on the outside looking in. We're just a bunch of losers."

Few people would argue with what Danny said. Built in 1928 as the district high school, the best days of Harpers Ferry were long gone before consolidation ate it up and turned it into a junior high school. Unlike Mecklenburg Junior High in the ritzy part of the county, our school didn't have a trophy case spilling over with trophies. And there weren't any banners or pictures dotting our hallways or hanging in the gym. There were no championship teams and nothing to remember. About the only thing we could count on was getting our butt kicked in every sport, every year.

"I'd sure like to beat those chest-pounding stuck-ups over at Mecklenburg in wrestling," Travis stated as we walked in late to our history class. He had moved to Harpers Ferry last summer with his mother and little brother and sister after his parents got divorced, and already he hated the ugly rivalry between the two schools. "Those jerks aren't content with just kicking our ass in sports. They have to rub it in. They have to sit back and laugh about it."

We all knew what Travis was talking about. We could remember only too well the 72-0 beating the Mecklenburg Lumberjacks had given our school last month in football. Their fans had laughed and chanted, *"Ya'll ain't nothing but Mountain Brats and River Rats! Mountain Brats and River Rats!"* It had hurt, and it was meant to hurt.

That's all we were to the Mecklenburg students. Nothing.

4

C oach Mac Waters and Jimmie Ray Lawson looked over our team during the second week of practice. "So what do you think of the team so far?" asked Coach Waters as we worked out in the cramped cafeteria.

"Good bunch of kids," mused Jimmie Ray, as everyone called our assistant coach. "But with so many starters gone, it'll be just like starting over," he said with a shake of his head. "We'll be right at the bottom, where things usually start out at Harpers Ferry."

Coach smiled at his buddy. They were a good combination. Jimmie Ray couldn't have stood more than five-foot four and was always laughing and smiling like a country boy getting his first taste of moonshine. Coach Waters was more serious, but how he could recruit the boys for wrestling! And come out we did. Even the people over at Mecklenburg didn't understand how our little school with two hundred twenty students could have more boys on our wrestling team than Mecklenburg did with an enrollment of over a thousand kids.

"At least you were able to get the Reynolds boy out for the team," said Jimmie Ray with satisfaction. He watched Stevie Reynolds easily manipulate a ninth grader who had been a starter the year before. Stevie had wrestled in the county youth league and won a peewee national championship when he was eight-years-old, so Coach had naturally assumed the little seventh grader with freckles and bright curly red hair would be eager to wrestle at Harpers Ferry. That had not been the case with Stevie Reynolds.

"I remember the first time I talked to him in the hallway," recalled Coach. "I went up and introduced myself and told him to be sure he had a physical before practice started. He just looked at me like I was crazy and told me he wasn't wrestling. It wasn't fun anymore. " Coach Waters frowned at the memory. "I'm telling you, Jimmie Ray, I thought I was going to crap myself right there in the hallway."

"What turned him against wrestling?"

"It was the youth league coaches," replied Coach. "I called his father and he told me it got to the point where Stevie hated wrestling. The coaches put too much pressure on him. If he made a mistake, they'd get in his face. Other times they'd totally ignore him if he lost. His father said he came home crying after practice too many times. They basically took all the fun out of it for him." He gave a satisfying nod as he watched Stevie practice his moves in fluid motion. "I promised his dad we'd make wrestling fun for him again."

Jimmie Ray kicked at the mat. "Never did like that youth league. They put too much damn pressure on the kids. Not like Little League where the kids just go out and have fun." It didn't help that most of the boys in the youth league were rich kids from the Mecklenburg school district. There was always a lot of trash talking from the adults, mostly about Harpers Ferry.

"I can't understand why there's so much bad blood between Mecklenburg and Harpers Ferry," reflected Coach. "It's almost like their kids are taught to hate us."

"It's the mentality of the people over at Mecklenburg," shrugged Jimmie Ray. "The kids think they're special. They look down on the Harpers Ferry kids as not good enough to asociate with. That's why they never shake hands with our kids after a game. It's like they don't want to dirty themselves."

Good things didn't come often to our West Virginia mountain town or to our little junior high school, which on the outside had the appearance of a cheerless prison. Our school boundary lines were conveniently drawn along the poor areas of the county, and included the homes that straddled the Potomac and Shenandoah Rivers and all of Blue Ridge Mountain. On the other side of Blue Ridge Mountain was Charles Town, home of Mecklenburg Junior High School. Charles Town had been founded in the 1700's by Charles Washington, brother of George, and was known for its many elegant homes, including five mansions that had been in the Washington family. It was where the rich people lived. Everything in our county revolved around Charles Town. The only thing that revolved around Harpers Ferry was hard times.

"By the way, what do you think of the Moore kid?" asked Coach, watching Tyler show Danny Schneider some basic moves. Danny had been cut from the basketball team and, with no other sport to play, had joined the wrestling team to the unending amusement of the rest of us. "I didn't realize he had cystic fibrosis when I asked him to come out for the team.

He sure doesn't like it when I tell him to take it easy on the wind sprints."

"He doesn't want any special favors," Jimmie Ray nodded towards Tyler. "Just wants to be treated like everyone else. Hell, he missed the whole first week of school back in August. When I asked the other students if he had moved away, the kids from Blue Ridge said he was probably in the hospital. Said it happened pretty often to him because of his illness." Jimmie Ray gave Tyler another appreciative look. "When he finally came to school he acted like it was no big deal, like it had never happened. Didn't want any fuss about it, that's for sure."

"I feel guilty telling him he could walk the halls as a champion if he came out for wrestling," said Coach, rubbing his chin as he studied Tyler. "The odds are really stacked against him. I don't see how he can make it."

"Don't count Tyler Moore out," said Jimmie Ray thoughtfully. "I know one thing about him already. The boy isn't a quitter."

5

"How come we're wrestling a middle school from Virginia?" asked Travis as we rolled out the mats for our opening match of the season. It was early December and the air had turned crisp. Already there was an early turnout of fans at the gym who buzzed excitedly about our chances for a successful season. "I thought junior highs didn't play middle schools in sports."

"I guess Coach wanted to give us an easy warm up before we wrestle the good schools," laughed Tyler, and everyone joined confidently in the laughing.

"I bet I could even win," chimed in Russell Perione, who knew he wouldn't be wrestling and that he wouldn't win if he did. He worked out regularly in practice with Tyler. He was the only boy that Tyler never had any trouble with.

The gym door opened and in strode the Aylor team. We stopped what we were doing and gawked at the boys as they walked to the locker room. Russell's mouth dropped open, and more than a few other seventh graders had their eyes turn into saucers. "For crying out loud! Did you see those guys?" asked Travis to no one in particular. "They look like they've been lifting weights all their life. I thought this was supposed to be an easy match!"

"I'm glad I'm not wrestling," mumbled Russell.

Chris Galford went out for Harpers Ferry in the first bout. It was his very first competitive wrestling match. He was a little blond-hair boy who weighed 60 pounds but was wrestling in the lowest weight class of 75 pounds. Chris was easily the smallest kid in the state but couldn't have cared less. Like Tyler Moore, he just wanted to get out on the mat and wrestle. He loved wrestling and hated to lose, even in practice. Though he was a very innocent-looking boy, you didn't mess with him when he was pissed off. The boy he had to wrestle made him look like a midget. He lunged at Chris on the whistle, taking him down and pinning him in one motion. It was over in a matter of seconds. Chris picked himself off the mat and gave the boy a slap handshake before stomping off the mat. Tears were streaming down his face. He never had a chance. "Damn!" he said, slinging his headgear to the floor.

The referee pointed an accusing finger at him and glanced at Coach Waters, shaking his head. "Warning, coach. Next time it'll cost you."

The scoring in wrestling is pretty simple. If a boy beats his opponent by seven points or less, called a simple decision, he earns three points for his team. A win by more than seven points, a major decision, is worth four team points, while a technical fall, a win by fifteen points, is good for five team points. The best you can do is to pin your opponent for six team points. Most matches are decided either by a pin or simple decision.

Chris went and sat down next to Scott Rinker, a ninth grader. "That wasn't fair!" he said sullenly, leaning back in his chair as he glared at his opponent. "That guy didn't even give me a chance to wrestle him!"

"Great sportsmanship you teach the boys, coach!" came a voice in the stands. "Just teach them how to wrestle and maybe they won't be such poor sports."

"Who are those guys?" asked Coach Waters irritably, looking up into the stands.

Jimmie Ray quickly scanned the top of the bleachers until his eyes settled on two men. "That's Lorenzo Fazzoli who's doing all the talking, a real jerk," Jimmie Ray told him. "He's up there with Dick Butcher, Mecklenburg's new assistant coach. Ignore them."

Both men were youth league wrestling coaches. Dick Butcher, while not a teacher in the county school system, had just been appointed as the new assistant coach of the Mecklenburg wrestling team. He was a big man, tall and rangy with a razor-thin mustache that gave him an intimidating appearance. Like many of the people who lived in Charles Town and ardently supported all the Mecklenburg sports programs, he was quite wealthy and used to getting his own way. He was a man who hated to lose more than anything in the world, and would often scream at his own son for making a mistake, even when the boy won a match. As Jimmie Ray would say, he was a man who thought he had no stink to himself.

The gym was much warmer that evening than the outside chill, and you could see the deep lines of Coach Waters' face speckled with sweat. "C'mon, Stevie, just remember what you did in practice. You'll swamp this guy," he shouted to our next wrestler, 80-pound Stevie Reynolds.

Stevie went out on the mat looking grossly overmatched against his much stronger Aylor opponent. Yet he worked the Aylor boy easily, and in the second period Little Red twisted him over on his back and pounced on his chest. Pin! The gym broke out in cheers as all of us went over to slap Stevie's hand.

"You're lucky the Reynolds boy already knew how to wrestle before you started coaching him!" floated down from the top of the stands.

Coach moved over to Tyler. He'd made the starting lineup at 85 pounds by default. The only other boy who weighed less, besides Chris Galford and Stevie, was Russell Perione.

"You can take this guy, Tyler," Coach told him hopefully. "If your breathing gets too rushed, let me know and I'll signal a timeout."

Tyler eyed our coach expectantly. "I don't need any timeout to help me get through," he said evenly, snapping his headgear under his chin.

As things turned out, Tyler didn't need a timeout for anything. His opponent wasted little time, pinning him in under twenty seconds. Tyler shook his opponent's hand and walked off the mat, dropping his headgear to the floor as he sat down. His eyes began to water. "Nice job of coaching!" wafted down from the stands. "He's a kid who's already supposed to know how to wrestle and he goes down like a creampuff! Yeah, he's learned a lot from you!" It came from Fazolli, and there was adult laughter from the little coaching contingent in the stands.

Tyler rubbed his eyes with his thumb and forefinger. His body began to jerk quietly back and forth as he tried to keep from crying. Coach Waters looked over at Danny and nodded to the locker room. "Let's get some water. It'll make you feel better," Danny said quietly. Tyler rose silently from his chair, his head still down as Danny nudged him to the locker room.

"Those damn bastards," muttered Coach after sending Scott Rinker out to wrestle at 90 pounds. He looked towards the stands. He knew Fazolli's comment had been directed at him, but it was Tyler who suffered the cutting words.

Tyler came out of the locker room a short time later and sat down next to Travis. "Tough match," offered Travis.

"Aw, hell, he was just lucky," Tyler informed him. "Anyhow, I'm over it." For the rest of the match he remained focused on cheering for his teammates, but there was little to cheer about. The highlight of the match had come much too early with Stevie Reynold's pin. We won only two more matches, both by more experienced ninth graders. The final score was 63-12.

"Harpers Ferry is always going to be a two-bit wrestling school until they get a *real* wrestling coach," came down from the stands. "You're an injustice to the kids, Waters, but we're not complaining!" This was met with great laughter at the top of the bleachers. The adult section.

After the match I stood outside the gym with Tyler, Danny, Travis and Jerry Wagner waiting for our ride home. Tyler's father had desperately wanted to see him wrestle but had to work late, and we were stuck in the cold night air contemplating whether we should start walking home. The moon was nearly full and the stars so bright it seemed like twilight. In the distance the Blue Ridge Mountain loomed over Harpers Ferry like a huge giant.

"We really got pasted tonight," began Jerry Wagner, a smart-mouthed eighth grader who spent most practices complaining and making excuses. "I'm not so sure about this wrestling stuff."

"But we could be champions one day," Tyler reminded him.

"You believe that crap? We're no good and it's too much hard work," Jerry said irritably, his breath popping out of his mouth. "I'm going to quit."

"You're stupid," said Tyler, shaking his head. "My dad taught me never to quit. He said a person who gives up when things get tough will never amount to anything. I may not be the greatest in wrestling or baseball, but you'll never see me quitting at *anything.*"

"You're a joke, Tyler! You're the one person who should quit everything! With your illness, *your disease,* you'll be damn lucky to make it through high school," seethed Jerry.

For a moment the air surrounding us seemed far more frozen than the falling temperatures. There was a quick flash from Danny's right arm, the sound of fist against bone, and Jerry fell to the pavement so quickly it was over before it seemed to happen. "Find your own way home, Wagner!" announced Danny, and we all turned and walked away, leaving Jerry Wagner lying in the parking lot.

Jerry Wagner quit the wrestling team the next day.

6

"**D**ig it out! No loafing on this team!" yelled Coach Waters, blowing his whistle for another wind sprint. We raced across the upstairs hallway at full speed and barely had time to catch our breath before he blew the whistle again. "One more sprint and down to the cafeteria!"

"He's killing us," complained Danny between gulps of air.

"Yeah, but we're winning now," said Evan Whalen as we made our way down the steps. At the bottom of the staircase, we were bowled over by the pungent smell of heavy body sweat coming from the cafeteria.

Tyler took in a deep breath. "Aw, the smell of men being men!" he laughed, walking into the cafeteria. "This is what living is all about!" Russell Perione was the only boy who held his nose.

"Okay, everyone in the cafeteria head upstairs for wind sprints. Players from upstairs grab a partner and start working on take-downs!" barked Jimmie Ray.

We groaned but hurried to the mats with our practice partners. Jimmie Ray would drill us non-stop on the different fundamentals as darkness slowly fell over the large cafeteria windows. Fifteen minutes later we would switch and go upstairs where Coach would run us to death with more wind sprints. The coaches never gave up and continued to push us, even when our team skidded to a 3-6 mark to open the season. Mecklenburg had whipped us easily before Christmas at their place, 56-24. Throughout the match their fans had laughed and chanted, *"Ya'll ain't nothing but Mountain Brats and River Rats! Mountain Brats and River Rats!"* God, how we hated them!

It was completely dark outside when Coach Waters brought his last group of sprinters down to the cafeteria. The routine never changed. Three hours of practice every day except game days. Don't miss practice and don't make excuses. What had started out so badly had turned into a successful season with our team winning thirteen of our last sixteen matches to improve to 16-9. Much of the success was due in large part to the transfer of Eddie Gilbert. He had moved to Harpers Ferry at the beginning of the season but wasn't eligible to wrestle until after Christmas.

"That boy has got to be the biggest flake I've ever seen in my life," remarked Coach as he and Jimmie Ray watched us go through our practice-ending calisthenics.

"No argument there," agreed Jimmie Ray. "But he just might be the best damn junior high wrestler I've ever seen."

Eddie Gilbert, a 110-pound eighth grader, had been wrestling as long as Stevie Reynolds and was every bit as good. Unlike Stevie, who was quiet and reserved, Eddie was outgoing and always looking for fun. But boy, he could wrestle, and with his goofy enthusiasm he lit a fire under our team. It was no accident that our team's resurgence came about at the same time that Eddie began reeling off his streak of sixteen straight pins.

He couldn't be beaten.

The season's last match was against Mecklenburg in front of the Harpers Ferry student body. Only two things remained unchanged from the beginning of the season. Tyler Moore still hadn't won his first match, and in twenty-five years Harpers Ferry still hadn't beaten Mecklenburg in a single sporting event. Maybe it really was because of John Brown's curse. Back when he tried to raid Harpers Ferry's arsenal was probably the only time we were important to anyone. The curse was a constant reminder that good things didn't come often to our small town.

The good folks of Harpers Ferry had discussed the curse many times.

"The last thing John Brown did before they hanged him over in Charles Town," they said, "was put a curse on Harpers Ferry for capturing him when he tried to start a slave rebellion."

"He was crazy for thinking he could free all the slaves and lead a revolt against all the white owners."

"The man was begging to be caught. When he saw his little revolt was going nowhere, he should have gotten out of town. Should have hold-up on the Blue Ridge Mountain," others would say.

"Who'd want to stay on the Blue Ridge Mountain?"

So John Brown and his band of vigilantes stayed in Harpers Ferry and were captured at the old firehouse. A month later they hanged him down the road in Charles Town, now home to the Mecklenburg Lumberjacks. Curious visitors would often ask why the curse wasn't put on the people of Charles Town instead of Harpers Ferry. Our local people would matter-of-factly tell them that it was John Brown's way of showing the injustices faced by different people, something we knew all about. "But," some of them would add rather proudly, "at least we can say that the Civil War was ignited right here in our little town."

The ironic thing is that while Harpers Ferry became famous, our home state of Virginia no longer wanted anything to do with us. The people up on Blue Ridge Mountain had to start a whole new state called West Virginia. It was like Harpers Ferry wasn't good enough for other people. That's how many of the folks up on Blue Ridge Mountain still felt.

The night before the Mecklenburg rematch, Coach Waters had knots in his stomach thinking about the possible lineup. But he knew one thing. The success of our team depended on what he did with Tyler Moore.

7

The next morning Coach didn't even tell Jimmie Ray of his plan. Everything had to fall into place perfectly, but as he reminded himself, we had nothing to lose. No one expected Harpers Ferry to win. Coach made his first move at lunch when he pulled Scott Rinker aside and whispered in his ear, "Now Scott, don't tell *anyone* about this, but here's what I want you to do..."

At 1:30 that afternoon our wrestling team assembled in the locker room to weigh in next to our Mecklenburg counterparts. The Mecklenburg wrestlers stood confidently as a group. Some had a look of contempt for our team. Others had smirks on their faces, arms folded across their chests as they waited impatiently to weigh in. "Look at the way those guys are trying to stare us down," whispered Danny to Tyler. "I've never seen such arrogance. It's like they can't wait to rub us into the ground."

"They're trying to psych us out, but it isn't going to work today," Tyler whispered back. "I think we can take them if we believe in ourselves. I know I do." Danny raised his eyebrows at his best friend but said nothing.

Chris Galford weighed in first at 75 pounds, drawing laughs for his small size from the Mecklenburg wrestlers. Chris stepped off the scales and clearly mouthed a profanity-laced message to a Mecklenburg boy twice his size. Stevie Reynolds was next at 80.

As Tyler stepped forward to weigh in at 85 pounds, Coach pulled him back. "Not you, Tyler. I'm going with Russell today."

The Harpers Ferry wrestlers suddenly became quiet. We looked at Coach like he had lost his mind. Tyler looked like he had just been bashed over the head, his eyes falling to the floor in total shock. True, the Mecklenburg kid had pinned him earlier in the season, but to remove him from the lineup for the last match was a slap in his face. Tyler may not have had as much to give as the other wrestlers, but he had always given everything he had. Everything. Always. None of us cared whether he won or lost. We just wanted him in the lineup.

"Hey, Coach," began Evan Whalen, our starting 135-pounder. "Tyler's been wrestling all year at 85 and..."

"Zip it!" said Coach curtly. "I'll make the decisions here! Russell! Get on the scales and weigh in!"

Jimmie Ray Lawson gave Coach a peculiar look but knew better than to question him in front of our team. Dick Butcher grinned over at his fellow Mecklenburg coach and said loud enough for everyone to hear, "Looks like a little problem with the team morale. How do you like that?" He was feeling good at the moment, very good. It would be a fun day.

Russell Perione was petrified. He carefully stepped up to the scales, his body noticeably shaking. "You doing all right, son?" asked the referee, sliding the weights on the scale.

"I kinda have an upset stomach," apologized Russell. "I don't know if I can wrestle."

"Just weigh in, Russell," said Coach sternly. "You've been waiting all year for this."

"I know, but my upset stomach..."

The rest of our team glanced over at Tyler. His face was beet red, but his eyes were dry. He stood stoically looking at the floor as our coach shamed him in front of his teammates. "Shit," muttered someone from the back of the locker room. We all knew it came from a Harpers Ferry wrestler. The Mecklenburg boys smirked at the unraveling of our team.

Russell Perione stepped off the scales and retreated to a corner. "All right, Scott! Get up there and weigh in at 90," Coach said without a hint of compassion. Scott had gotten much better from wrestling with Stevie Reynolds in practice and had pinned Mecklenburg's 90-pounder back in December. But Scott had also wrestled with Tyler in many practices, making Tyler a better wrestler each time they worked out. Everyone could see the improvement in Tyler, even if Coach Waters couldn't. "How's the shoulder feeling, Scott?" asked Coach as he stepped away from the scales.

Scott played his role exactly the way Coach had told him. "It's real sore, Coach. I can barely lift my arm." Dick Butcher and the Mecklenburg head coach smiled at each other.

Coach shook his head. "Tyler! Can you wrestle?" he asked with loud exaggeration.

Tyler clenched his teeth tightly. He had something to prove now. He'd show Coach if he could wrestle! Coach looked over at Mecklenburg's pudgy 90-pounder. There wasn't an ounce of muscle on him. Yes, Tyler could take him. There had never been a doubt in his mind. "Go weigh in then."

"You already weighed one boy in, coach," said Butcher. "You can't wrestle two at once," he laughed cynically.

"No rule says I can't weigh in another one." The referee shrugged with indifference as Tyler got on the scales.

When we got to the 110-pound weight class, Mecklenburg got careless. Their boy was a cream puff who had won by forfeit in December when we didn't have anyone to wrestle at that weight. That wouldn't happen again. We now had Eddie Gilbert at 110, and no one was going to beat him. "Why give the Harpers Ferry fans a thrill by letting them see Gilbert slam our kid with a quick pin?" Butcher asked with an air of knowledge. "We'll forfeit the weight since they don't have anyone to wrestle at 116. It'll be like trading points." He knew what he was talking about. "No big deal."

After Eddie weighed in at 110 pounds, the referee moved to 116. Coach carefully scraped at the floor with his shoe. All the pieces of the puzzle had fallen together. Now it was up to the kids.

"Not entering anyone at 116?" Butcher asked sarcastically.

Coach looked over at Mecklenburg's stud. "Don't have any-one to make it a match," he said with resignation.

Butcher smiled and turned to the other coach. "I'm going to enjoy sweeping the season's two matches from this joke of a coach. He doesn't know crap about wrestling."

8

C hris Galford was still steaming from being laughed at during the weigh ins and wrestled on anger-filled adrenaline. He wasn't a kid to be messed with when he was mad, and he was plenty mad that afternoon. Despite being badly overmatched, he squirmed out a hard-fought 4-2 win. Stevie Reynolds followed with his fifteenth pin of the season. The Harpers Ferry gym was rocking like it had never rocked before, but it was still early. That was evident when Russell Perione was quickly pinned in a near-record ten seconds.

"I don't know what the hell their coach was thinking by wrestling that kid," laughed Dick Butcher to his good buddy Lorenzo Fazolli, who had joined him behind the team bench. "He doesn't know the first thing about strategy." Fazolli laughed heartily. They were ready to enjoy the rest of the match.

When Tyler Moore checked in to wrestle at 90 pounds, Butcher never saw the way things were going to unfold. Coach had known since last night that Tyler would be like a wounded animal if he was snubbed at 85 and moved to 90 out of sheer necessity. But Coach also had complete faith that Tyler would rise to the occasion. He knew Tyler's makeup as a person. He knew that when everything was on the line, Tyler had all the *intangibles* to be a winner.

"Tyler, you can take this boy. Just stay low and shoot for an opening," Coach said, leading him to the mat.

"I can take him," said Tyler angrily, gritting his teeth, not realizing the entire weigh in scenario had been carefully planned in advance. "You just wait! I'll show you I can wrestle!"

Tyler did wrestle that afternoon. He moved at the whistle, taking his opponent down in a frenzy. "Run it, Tyler! Turn him and run it!" shouted Jimmie Ray from the side of the mat, sensing something wonderful in the making.

Tyler slipped his arm under his opponent's armpit. His heels dug into the mat to gain leverage. "Now, Tyler! Now! Turn him!" yelled Jimmie Ray, jumping up and down like a madman.

Tyler grunted as he struggled to turn over his heavier opponent, never letting up even as the boy cried out in pain. With one last mighty heave, he flipped the Mecklenburg boy over on his back. Tyler drove the boy's shoulders into the mat, one arm cradled under his neck, his other arm locking the boy's shoulder. "Squeeze him, Tyler! Squeeze him!" Jimmie Ray screamed. "You can do it, boy!"

The referee's hand came up in a wide arc and slammed to the mat. Pin! Tyler had won! Tyler jumped up and rocketed toward the ceiling, his outstretched right arm nearly touching the rafters. The ref grabbed his left arm and motioned him to the center circle. Tyler shook hands with the Mecklenburg wrestler and quickly turned around. His father had come down from the stands and Tyler ran towards him, flying through the air. Mr. Moore stretched out his arms and caught Tyler as he wrapped his legs around his father's waist. He pointed his fist high into the air. The two hugged as the crowd went wild, cheering and clapping in the most spectacular show of love and affection and craziness ever seen in our gym. Mr. Moore was still spinning Tyler around on his waist when Tyler caught Coach's eyes. Coach simply nodded and gave Tyler a thumbs up. Tyler's face lit up into a smile that crossed from one ear to the other, his arm extended towards Coach, his thumb also in the air.

For Dick Butcher at this point, there was little cause for concern. After all, the Rinker kid would have scored a pin, too. It was only when Scott Rinker approached the scorer's table to check in for the next match, flexing his arms with a confidant smile, did the look on Butcher's face become drawn and serious.

"You can't do that!" he screamed, charging toward the scorer's table.

"Our boy's feeling much better and wants to wrestle," said Coach nonchalantly. "He weighed in at 90; I can bump him up to 95. Check the rules."

It was a pivotal match. The Mecklenburg boy was tough and had manhandled Danny Schneider back in December, but Coach believed that Scott could step up and take him. His confidence in Scott was not lost. The months of rugged practice paid off, with Scott winning a thrilling 6- 5 decision that left both boys gasping for breath. The gym rocked with screams that made mothers cover their ears.

Coach kneeled down next to Danny Schneider, our usual 95-pounder who had won only eight matches all year. "Here's what I want you to do, Danny," Coach explained to him. "I want you to take one for the team and move up to the 102-pound match."

"I can't, Coach, that guy's good!" he argued. "He'll kill me!"

Maybe Danny didn't understand Coach's reasoning, but the look that crossed Butcher's face told a different story. He was beginning to get the big picture. He stared across the gym at Coach Waters like an animal that has just been cornered with no way out. "YOU CAN'T DO THAT!" he yelled as Danny checked in. "That boy weighed in at 95 pounds! He can't wrestle 102!"

Even Jimmie Ray understood now as he walked over to the scorer's table with a huge grin. Jimmie Ray was known as a master referee before becoming a coach, the highest rated ref in the tri-state area. Everyone knew his knowledge of the rules was superior. His integrity was held in even higher esteem.

"Coach Waters is playing by the rules," he said knowingly, catching the nervous face of Butcher. "He can bump up any wrestler one weight class, and I believe he's playing a bump-up game like I've never seen before." He gave Coach a smile of genuine admiration.

Danny went down like a good soldier, getting pinned quickly by his opponent. Coach then bumped up our regular 102-pounder, Cody Harris, to the 110-pound weight. Cody wasn't a much better wrestler than Danny, but in their smugness the Mecklenburg coaches had conceded the 110-pound weight class to Eddie Gilbert. Now Cody moved up to accept the forfeit. Suddenly the entire gym understood that Eddie would be moved up to wrestle Mecklenburg's 116-pound stud that only he could beat.

When Cody checked in for the 110-pound match, Butcher rushed over to the scorer's table and waved frantically to his 116-pound wrestler. The ref shook his head and waved the other way. "C'mon, coach, you weighed the boy in at 116. You know you can't move him down. What are you trying to do here?" He motioned Cody to the center of the mat to accept the forfeit, raising his arm in victory. Cody grinned at winning an unexpected match, the crowd cheering him on while Butcher could only spit syllables of words in anger.

Coach went over to Eddie Gilbert. "This is what you've been waiting for, Eddie."

"No kidding," agreed Eddie with an air of cockiness. He stood up and handed the Coke he was drinking to Stevie Reynolds. "Don't let it get warm. I'll be right back," he cracked as he took off his warmup.

Eddie and the Mecklenburg stud walked over to the scorer's table. Eddie was grinning like a hyena. He feared nothing, and the gym, the fans, the screaming, were all his. He lived for this, and the gym was his stage. "Are you boys ready?" asked the referee as the boys positioned themselves for the whistle.

"You bet I'm ready," grinned Eddie, looking his opponent straight in the eye. The Mecklenburg boy knew he was now the underdog and wrestled like one. Eddie kept coming at him, pounding, pounding. It didn't take long to get the kid on his back. Pandemonium broke loose when Eddie leveled the boy's shoulders to the mat for a pin.

Coach jumped up with both arms raised, and the gym followed his lead with a deafening roar. With the score already 30-12, it looked like a stunning Harpers Ferry upset. But things were barely getting warmed up. There was more to come, lots more.

9

"**D**on't reach back! Don't reach back!" screamed Coach Waters as the Mecklenburg wrestler controlled our 155-pounder. But our wrestler didn't hear him and reached his arm backward to try and grab his opponent. The Mecklenburg kid quickly hooked his arm under our boy and turned him on his back, and just like that, it was over. Another Mecklenburg pin.

"For *chrissake!*" yelled Coach. "We're trying to *give* this match away! Can't anyone do what they're told?"

"We're still ahead, Mac" said Jimmie Ray, looking up at the scoreboard. Mecklenburg had come roaring back from a 39-18 deficit to score two quick pins, and with two matches remaining had closed the gap to 39-30.

"If we don't take the next match, we can hang it up!" said Coach. He knew that after the 165-pound bout, we would be sending up Artie Badger, a 170-pound seventh grader against Mecklenburg's undefeated heavyweight. Artie was a tough kid who would go to hell and bring back fire if the coaches asked him, but he would be no match for the Mecklenburg ninth-grader.

"No!" screamed Coach as our 165-pounder was splayed out on his back and pinned. The Mecklenburg crowd stood as one, clapping and cheering as the Harpers Ferry student body fell silent, their eyes on Artie Badger. He was too small to be wrestling heavyweight.

Coach went over and placed his hand on Artie's shoulder. "Now listen, Artie, play defense and keep away from this guy," he said as Artie adjusted his headgear. "If this guy pins you, we lose." Artie's hazel eyes were expressionless as he nodded.

A lot of junior high heavyweights are butterballs, more fat than muscle. But the Mecklenburg boy was no butterball; he was 230 pounds of rock hard muscle with Godzillian strength. He already had hair sprouting on his face with a front tooth out. The boy was downright mean and nasty looking. He went out to meet Artie with a snarl between deep-set eyes. There would be no fooling around.

"Just pin him and we go home winners," yelled Butcher confidently in front of the Mecklenburg bench. The Harpers Ferry lead had shrunk to 39-36. The best we could hope for was that Godzilla wouldn't pin Artie and the match would end in a tie. But everyone was expecting a quick pin.

Twice Godzilla had Artie on his back, but both times he survived getting pinned, once by crawling out of bounds and the second time when the buzzer ended the second period. There were only twelve seconds left in the third and final period when Godzilla got on top of Artie again. He pressed Artie's shoulders to the mat and nearly had him pinned, the score 15-8, the final seconds counting off.

"Fight him, Artie! Don't give up!" screamed Coach. The referee's hand started to come down. Three, two, one. The buzzer sounded.

For a moment no one moved. Had the ref's hand hit the mat? Was Artie pinned? The referee stood up, motioned the pin had come too late and signaled the Mecklenburg wrestler the winner, 15-8. The overall match had ended in a dead draw.

"A tie hurts, but it's damn better than a loss," Coach said with a sigh to Jimmie Ray. He crossed the length of the gym to congratulate the Mecklenburg coaches and called out to Butcher. "Nice match, coach. Want to set up some exhibition matches for the other boys?" He extended his hand to Butcher.

The Mecklenburg coach knocked Coach's hand away. "We're not wrestling any exhibition matches and we're sure as hell not wrestling Harpers Ferry again!" he roared, saliva flying from his mouth as he poked a finger in Coach's chest. "You were a bunch of piss-ass cheaters in the lower weights!"

"You don't know what you're talking about!" Coach fired back, turning away. "Maybe if you learned the rules, you'd learn something about strategy! We play by the book!"

Butcher jumped back in front of Coach. "You little pisser!" he sneered. "I know more about wrestling than you'll learn in a lifetime!" The Mecklenburg wrestlers began crowding around the coaches, taking in the conversation.

Suddenly a roar went up from the crowd. People began shouting. Coach wheeled around and saw the referee throw up his hands. He was pointing to Godzilla and holding up one finger. Godzilla was cussing like crazy. The ref shook his head and raced over to the scorer's table with Godzilla dogging him. The scorer nodded and subtracted a point off the scoreboard.

"Your heavyweight isn't going to cuss me out, coach! He's being flagged for unsportsmanlike conduct! I'm not taking that kind of lip from some fifteen-year-old!" he said emphatically to Butcher. "That's one point off your team score!" Butcher looked up at the scoreboard lights blazing the final score, *"Harpers Ferry 39, Visitors 38."*

The Mecklenburg wrestlers began pushing around some of our smaller wrestlers. Tempers were flaring. Jimmie Ray ran through the crowd and began tossing aside Mecklenburg wrestlers twice his size. He reached out and grabbed Chris Galford, who was surrounded by Mecklenburg wrestlers but still giving each of them a piece of his mind. Jimmie Ray dragged him through the yelling throng as Chris continued firing more insults over his shoulder.

A couple of the Mecklenburg adults had spilled out on the floor and joined Godzilla in jawing with the ref. It was ugly. Their wrestler was swearing at the referee like there wasn't any tomorrow, and their adults were acting like six-year-olds because a call hadn't gone their way.

The Mecklenburg coaching staff had been beaten by their own arrogance, and the curse of John Brown had been laid to rest. We had finished the season with a 17-9 record. It was the most wins our junior high school had ever achieved in any sport. We knew Harpers Ferry would never look back again.

Part Two
Eighth Grade
10

The nail-biting victory over Mecklenburg paid huge dividends the following school year. More than forty boys came out for the team, all of them eager to wrestle. Jimmie Ray was already putting us through calisthenics when Coach Waters joined him in the cafeteria. A cool November breeze flowed through the open windows. "I just talked with Mr. Crawford," Coach said with a smile. "He's going to ask the school board for another paid assistant coach to help us."

"I thought he didn't think we needed one." Mr. Crawford was the principal and didn't like asking the board office for things he considered unnecessary. Money was needed for far more important things at the county's poorest school.

"I had to go over Mr. Crawford's head," admitted Coach. "I called Wayne, Dixie and Paul with the alumni association and explained how Ben Duval has two assistant coaches to help him coach twenty-five boys in football, while it's just the two of us for wrestling." Ben Duval was the longtime athletic director and coached all the boys' varsity sports except wrestling. He had always hated the curse of John Brown.

Jimmie Ray grinned. "And I suppose the gentlemen used some strong-arm tactics?"

Coach nodded. "They flipped when I told them we have forty-two boys out for wrestling. They said we're the pride and joy of the alumni association, that it's nice to finally have a winning team here at the old school. They called Mr. Crawford and said if he expected to get any more money from the alumni, he damn sure better get us another coach."

It was true. The alumni association contributed a great deal of money to both the school and the athletic department. Their financial support was needed for everything from new uniforms to office equipment to helping the poorer students out at Thanksgiving and Christmas. Most of the alumni were in their sixties or even older, from the glory days when Harpers Ferry did pretty well in sports and actually won a few trophies. It didn't matter that their old school was now a junior high. They still religiously supported it because it still bore the Harpers Ferry name, the same as when it was a high school for less than one hundred fifty students in grades seven through twelve before consolidation. The ancient school and the memories that went with it were the only thing that some of the old gents had left.

"You still want to ask Lenny Langston to be our coach?" wondered Jimmie Ray.

"He knows his stuff," Coach answered.

Lenny had learned to wrestle from his older brother and Dick Butcher in the youth league. When he was in the ninth grade, Coach and Jimmie Ray started the wrestling program at Harpers Ferry. He was already an accomplished wrestler by then and easily went undefeated at Harpers Ferry, then capped off his wrestling career with a runner-up state finish in high school. If the coaches had one knock on Lenny, it was that he didn't show them much respect. Instead of listening to his own coaches during a match, Lenny would ignore them and look up into the stands for guidance from his brother who, like Butcher, didn't think much of Mac Waters and Jimmie Ray. But Lenny was out of school now and presumably more mature. It would be a chance for him to pass along his skills and knowledge to the younger boys.

"Yeah, Mr. Waters, I'd love to help you and Mr. Lawson coach wrestling," Lenny said excitedly that night when Coach called him. "I'd like to get into coaching when I graduate from college. This will be a great experience for me!"

"It won't interfere with your classes? You'll be able to go on a few weekend trips with us?" Coach questioned.

"Don't worry about that," Lenny assured him. "You guys were good to me at Harpers Ferry. This will be a chance to pay you back." Lenny was fairly gushing.

Two days later Ben Duval stopped Coach Waters in the hallway. He said that Lenny Langston couldn't be approved as their new wrestling coach. Mecklenburg had turned in his name to be a paid assistant coach the day before, and Lenny had accepted. He had called his older brother to tell him about his offer to coach at Harpers Ferry, and his brother had promptly called Dick Butcher. With a little bad-mouthing of Harpers Ferry, the two of them had been able to convince Lenny that he would be much better off coaching at Mecklenburg. After all, if Harpers Ferry was going to have three paid coaches, then Mecklenburg damn well was, too.

That night Coach called Lenny again and begged and pleaded with him to return to his old school. Nothing he could say could undo all of Butcher's trash talking about Harpers Ferry. To Coach, Lenny Langston was now a traitor. To Dick Butcher, it was time to smile. Paybacks were hell.

* * * * *

"Maybe it's for the best the way things turned out," Jimmie Ray remarked thoughtfully to Coach Waters. They were watching Tyler Moore's father lead the team through an early December practice in the cafeteria. Though Coach Waters was still bitter over the Lenny Langston fiasco, he agreed that Bill was a good fit for the team. When Big Bill stood next to little Tyler, it was hard to believe they were father and son. Tyler's weight was now at 90 pounds, but he was still weak and thin-looking from the effects of cystic fibrosis. If Tyler's mother had her way, he would never wrestle again. But Bill insisted his only boy be treated the same as any other kid, which is just the way Tyler wanted it. Big Bill didn't cut him any favors because of his illness.

"Tyler, you knucklehead!" roared Bill. "How many times have I told you not to reach back to grab your opponent? Get upstairs and run ten wind sprints, and run them hard!" he commanded.

"*I always do!*" Tyler said defiantly, leaving the cafeteria.

11

"How do you think we'll do this weekend?" Jimmie Ray asked Coach Waters on Friday morning. We were throwing our gear into cars and trucks for our first overnight trip of the season.

"We've got a nice bunch of seventh graders to go with our eighth graders," he observed. "I wish we had a few more ninth graders to provide some leadership. Eddie Gilbert is a great wrestler, but he's not exactly a leader when it comes to common sense."

Jimmie Ray chuckled. So what if Eddie was a bit of an airhead? The boy could wrestle. "I think this is the year we start running with the big dogs in the state instead of just chasing them. This weekend will be a good measuring stick for us," he said. "Oh, yeah, you might as well hear the bad news now. I heard through the grapevine this morning that Mecklenburg is going to Wheeling, too."

At 9:00 the convoy of cars, trucks and vans driven by parents pulled out of the parking lot for the four-hour trip to Wheeling. The coaches liked having as many parents as possible on these trips, promising them a free stay if they were willing to sleep in a room with three boys. That was asking a lot. But this not only solved our transportation problem, it also provided much-needed chaperones. Our team had opened the season by crushing Aylor Middle School a few days earlier, and expectations were high for the school's first twenty-win season.

* * * * *

"It's always a rush walking in here," commented Coach as he and Jimmie Ray led our team into the Sherrard Junior High gym. It seemed absolutely cavernous with five large wrestling mats occupying all available floor space. The bleachers on both sides of the gym had been pulled out and filled to capacity with screaming junior high kids and adults. It was more like an arena than a gym.

The coaches turned toward the side of the main entrance where the Sherrard team had just emerged. The boys walked confidently as they traveled the length of the gym in single file, their gray warm-ups giving the allusion of a long, gray line that seemed to go on forever. It was very intimidating, and the home crowd roared its approval. "I love the way they parade in here before the tournament," Coach deadpanned. "I think it psyches out a lot of teams."

"The first year we saw them do that, half our kids were afraid to get on the mats with them," laughed Jimmie Ray. "We were beaten the moment we saw them."

Coach cocked his head to the side as he studied the powerfully built gray line move past him. "They're good all right," he agreed. "But each year we get a little closer to beating them. Maybe this will be the year."

"Hey, coach! Great to see you! So glad you guys made it up!" greeted Ralph Barnett, the Sherrard coach. He poked

Coach playfully on the arm. "You guys always scare me. You're the team to beat! You're tough!"

Coach laughed as he shook hands. He liked Coach Barnett. Always full of bullshit. He was perhaps the best coach in the state and had an easygoing manner that naturally drew people to him. He stood there grinning at Coach with a lopsided smile, his glass eye staring off crazily in the opposite direction of his real eye. It was sort of embarrassing. Most people couldn't tell the real one from the fake one and didn't know which one to look at.

Our first match was against Tucker County. "Look at our seventh graders," Tyler nudged at Danny Schneider before the match. He was leaning back in his folding chair like a seasoned veteran, his legs stretched out in front of him. "They're all looking over at the Tucker County team, trying to figure out who they're going to wrestle. You can tell they're nervous. Me? I don't care who I wrestle," he said confidently.

Danny rolled his eyes. "You won one match last year, Tyler," he reminded him.

"Yeah, but it was the last match of the season when the team needed me the most," he said proudly.

Chris Galford was back as an eighth grader, weighing all of 65 pounds, and again the smallest wrestler in the state. Coach and Jimmie Ray had started calling him the *"Little Beast"* because he feared no one. He promptly showed why in the first match by reaching up behind his taller opponent's neck, locking his hands under the boy's shoulder and then twisting around as he flipped the boy over. Chris pounced on the stunned boy's chest as the referee quickly counted one, two, three, and the match was over.

"He called me a squirt before the match," Chris said smugly, sitting down next to Stevie Reynolds.

Seventh grader Ronnie Dillow followed next at 80 pounds. He wasn't as strong as most boys, but he used skill and technique to offset this deficit. Ronnie quickly scored a take-down on his opponent, and then controlled him as the boy thrashed around trying to escape. Ronnie couldn't put the kid away and pin him, but by the end of the third period the boy was worn-out and eventually fell by an 8-3 score.

After that our team couldn't be stopped. We won nine of the next thirteen matches. Only Tyler and Tommy Johnson lost in the lower weight classes. In the upper weight classes, the two other starting ninth graders besides Eddie Gilbert also lost. But the mood was set.

After the win against Tucker County, our team cruised to successive wins over Cameron and Grant County before finally being upended by a powerful Independence squad, 43-37. Independence had arrived late for the tournament due to a snowstorm along the mountain ridges, and their arrival had shuffled some of the matches around with delayed starting times. When a wrestler suffered a neck injury during the fourth round, play was suspended while officials waited for an ambulance. By the time we finished wrestling Independence it was 11:30 at night. All the wrestling was over except for the last remaining match between Harpers Ferry and Edison.

"You're not going to make us wrestle tonight, are you, Ralph?" questioned Coach Waters.

"Sorry, Coach," he said apologetically. "You know you can't wrestle six matches tomorrow. It's against the rules. You've got to get it in tonight, or it'll throw everything out of whack. My hands are tied. They really are."

The other teams packed their belongings and left the gym. Coach Waters and Jimmie Ray were left muttering at the ugly thought of wrestling Edison with an exhausted bunch of boys. True, the Edison team was tired, too, but they only had to motor forty-five minutes down the highway, not four hours like we had done. Coach Barnett turned off the back lights. The gym suddenly had a peculiar, eerie feeling as a silence fell over it with the departure of everyone else. The only lights on were the ones above the mat.

"I'm going back to the hotel," grumbled a ninth grader who knew he wouldn't be wrestling. "I don't want to stay for this." Two of the parents had volunteered to drive kids who weren't wrestling back to the hotel.

Some of the starting wrestlers rolled their eyes as a few of our teammates started to collect their gear. Not Tyler. "Where are you guys goings? Are you crazy?" he asked with a look of total disbelief. He pointed to the ninth grader. "We're a team. We all want to wrestle, but we're a team first." His tone seemed to question the boy's concept of being a team. "Hell, I don't feel like a contributing member of the team the way I'm wrestling," Tyler said, having won only one of his four matches that day.

"But we've got to pick each other up. Would you go to bed early if your favorite football team was playing on TV?"

The ninth grader studied Tyler's expression for a moment, then flicked his hands in the air and nodded. "Yeah, good point. You're right." He smiled with resignation and sat back down. All the other boys sat back down with him.

Coach Waters grinned at Tyler's father. "Your boy has a way of getting others to listen to him. I like that."

"I wish the little knucklehead would listen to me. He always wants to run the damn show."

Coach turned toward his wrestlers. "All right, boys, let's get ready to wrestle!" he said, pumping his hand in the air. The emptiness of the gym made his words bounce off the walls as Chris Galford went out for the first match. It was a few minutes after midnight. Wrestlers on both teams huddled together on opposite sides of the mat, afraid they might be swallowed up in the surrounding darkness. Even the parents had silently crept down from the darkened bleachers to stand under the lights. It was very surreal.

Edison had a full contingent of wrestlers for each weight class, and though we easily handled them, the match dragged on for over an hour. It was nearly 1:30 in the morning when our team left the gym, and it would be another half-hour before we got back to the hotel after finding a fast-food place.

Everyone was ready for bed except Eddie Gilbert.

12

We picked up where we left off the next day, sweeping our first three matches in the morning to run our record to 7-1. Our next match was against Sherrard, a team that had always dominated us in the past. We'd have to close the tournament against Mecklenburg, and everyone knew it was going to be a long ride home for the loser.

We started out evenly against Sherrard as the *Little Beast* won, Ronnie Dillow lost, Stevie pinned, and Tyler got pinned. But both Travis and Danny pulled off pins, and suddenly we were in the driver's seat with our most dominating wrestler, Eddie Gilbert, scheduled to wrestle next. Funny thing, though. Eddie was nowhere to be seen.

"Where's Gilbert?" screamed Coach Waters as players went scurrying to the locker rooms, bathrooms, hallways, concession areas, anywhere that Eddie might be. But Mr. Flake was nowhere to be found.

Eddie was a ninth grader now, and it was like a pretty picture when he'd pull off one of those slick, fancy moves no one had ever seen before. Counting last year, he had a streak of twenty-six straight pins. No one could imagine him ever losing. Unfortunately, Eddie had a penchant for leading himself, and anyone with him, down the wrong path. Not intentionally. It just came naturally to him. He and common sense just didn't get along.

The night before, when the team had gotten back to the hotel, most people couldn't wait to drop into bed. Not Eddie. Anytime was a good time for a party. "Give me five minutes and we'll be in paradise," he said confidently, pulling wires from the back of the television.

The other three boys in the room—the only room without an adult—looked at Eddie curiously. "What are you doing, Eddie?" asked Evan Whalen. "I want to go to bed."

"Forget it. I'm going to give you guys an education," he said smugly. "I saw where you can buy x-rated movies for the TV, and I know how to circumvent the wires. Of course I know all about this x-rated stuff, done some of it myself actually, but you guys might learn a thing or two," he added gleefully.

The other boys stayed up bug-eyed while Eddie did his best to explain, and take in, what was new to him, too. They eventually drifted off to sleep after the initial excitement wore off, except for Eddie, who was mesmerized watching the real deal for the first time. When the show was over, Eddie thought a little snack would be in order, so he snuck out to an all-night diner across from the motel. He came back and plopped in bed to finish off a second Coke, spilling it over Evan Whalen sleeping next to him. Evan woke up with a loud scream, his cussing and yelling waking up everyone in the next room. One of the parents began pounding on the door, which Eddie answered with an innocent grin. "Evan just woke up and thought he'd peed himself, but he's all cleaned up now," he offered sheepishly. It was five in the morning when everyone got back to sleep, with Evan on the floor. Eddie didn't mind the wet bed, but the wakeup call two hours later was a different story.

"Where the hell is Gilbert?" demanded Coach when no one could find him. The idea that Eddie would be afraid to wrestle anyone was incomprehensible. Coach stalled for as long as he could. Finally the ref raised his opponent's arm into the air to signal the forfeit. We had just let a golden opportunity slip away.

The match was almost over when Ronnie Dillow pointed up into the bleachers and said softly, almost reverently, "Look, there's Eddie." It was like he had just seen The Resurrection. Everyone followed Ronnie's arm. Eddie's head was poking above one of the upper bleacher steps where he'd been sleeping peacefully out of sight.

Eddie made his way down the bleachers, rubbing sleep from his eyes. "When is it my turn to wrestle?" he asked. "I'm ready to go!"

Coach Waters began making gurgling sounds but nothing came out. Jimmie Ray quickly stepped in front of him and said quietly, "Go take one of your pills, Mac. Let me handle this."

Coach Waters could get very uptight during the matches. He was always worrying about something. Prescription pills helped settle his nerves. We called them his happy pills.

Travis laughed. "Coach is ready to tear Eddie apart right now."

"Yeah, but after he takes his happy pill, he'll be fine," said Tyler.

Danny agreed. "No kidding. Once it kicks in, he and Eddie will be like best buddies."

Our eyes followed Coach as he walked to a water fountain and washed a pill down. We couldn't help but giggle.

Jimmie Ray looked at Eddie and shook his head. "You just let your team down, boy. You ought to feel real proud of yourself." He turned around and watched Artie Badger pin his opponent in the last bout, but the match had already been decided. Harpers Ferry lost, 46-38.

Coach was feeling better when he returned to the mat. The pill was working. "If we can beat Mecklenburg, we can still take second or third place, depending on how the tie-breakers work out," he said, penciling in his lineup.

"You're not thinking of wrestling Gilbert?"

"I'm over it," he replied. "I want to win this match and take home a trophy."

Jimmie Ray shook his head. "Don't do it, Mac. If you go ahead and wrestle Gilbert, you'll be sending the wrong message to the kids. He's got to be held accountable for what he did, accident or not." He shook his head again. "I want to win as bad as you, but this isn't the way to do it."

Coach stared at the lineup on his clipboard. He scratched at his temple. "Hell, Jimmie Ray, if it was any other team but Mecklenburg."

"Don't do it, Mac," advised Jimmie Ray again. "You're the head coach and it's your call, but it's also a matter of principle. Are the boys going to respect you for allowing someone to let the team down without any consequences?" He shrugged. "You're almost sounding like Butcher. Win at any cost."

Coach shook his head and erased Eddie's name from the lineup. In the end it really didn't matter. The emotional loss to Sherrard had sucked the wind from us, and the long hours from the night before began to take its toll. We were a tired, beaten bunch before the match even started. "All I want to do is go to sleep," mumbled one boy, his eyes closed.

But to one boy, the match did matter. It was Tyler Moore. "We can take Mecklenburg! We can beat them today!" he kept repeating to us, walking up and down the long row of chairs where we sat. "You've got to believe in yourselves! We can do it!"

His words fell on deaf ears. Mecklenburg won going away, 54-27. Evan Whalen, complaining of a sore back all day, was pinned. So was Tommy Johnson. Ditto for Travis Nutter. Throw in Eddie Gilbert for not even wrestling. Four wrestlers in the same room. All of them losing by pin or forfeit. They weren't a pretty sight.

And then there was Tyler. He had given the tournament everything his body could muster. But unlike the other wrestlers who leaned back in their chairs after getting pinned or badly beaten, their eyes closed, dreaming of sleep, Tyler's eyes never left the floor beneath him. His head was in his hands. The coaches had been depending on him to set an early tone by pinning the kid he had stuffed last year. It was a chance for him to step up and be a contributing part of the team. And he had lost. He had let the team down. He had let the coaches down. It wasn't something to take lightly.

13

Although our team finished a disappointing fourth at the Sherrard tournament, we did learn one thing about ourselves. We could compete with anyone and, with a little bit more luck and a little more self-discipline, we could have won the whole tournament. There was no finger-pointing, however. Eddie Gilbert had apologized to the entire team for, in his own words, *"Being so gosh darn pooped out and falling asleep,"* and his apology had been accepted.

Tyler was really the only wrestler who bore any guilt. It was because his inner drive to achieve and to be accepted as a regular kid was so great. To the rest of us on the team, he was already an inspiration, but it was difficult to praise him when all he wanted to be was like everyone else. Our team came back from Wheeling with a sense of purpose and an even more determined attitude to succeed.

The following Tuesday we thrashed Warm Springs, our neighbor two counties over, by a 66-12 score, and then traveled to Buckhannon on the weekend to close out our December schedule. We pretty much destroyed everyone in the field except Independence, who beat us again, 43-35. It was a tough loss to swallow, but at least we finished second to finally come home with a trophy. Maybe not a championship trophy, but a trophy just the same.

The memory of the stinging back-to-back losses to Sherrard and Mecklenburg began to fade, replaced by a desire to achieve something as yet undefined. It was a feeling that excited the team, especially Tyler.

*   *   *   *   *

Four days after we returned to school in January, we squared off against Mecklenburg in front of the Harpers Ferry student body. The only thing different from the year before was that there was now a police officer in the gym. Harpers Ferry stood 13-4 and Mecklenburg 12-2, and everyone in the county knew it would be a battle. No one was let down. It was a close match with the lead constantly swinging back and forth. When Mecklenburg took the 165 pound weight class with only the heavyweight bout left, we held a slim one-point lead, 37-36. But this time there would be no Godzilla for Artie Badger to wrestle, and Artie easily took his opponent down for a match-ending pin. And unlike last year, we didn't consider the win to be an upset. We were good now, and we knew it.

We swept three more matches from nearby Maryland and Virginia teams by lopsided scores before traveling to Braxton County for our last overnight trip. It was a six-team tournament where we splintered the competition by winning four of five matches. Our only loss came to perennial state power McKinley, but at least we won another runner-up trophy. If we weren't one of the big dogs yet, our 21-5 record showed we were at least running with them. Still ahead was a rematch in front of the

Mecklenburg student body and a season-ending tournament at the county high school.

* * * * *

We were leaving the cafeteria after practice the night before our match with Mecklenburg when Coach overheard Tyler talking with Danny and Travis. "Yeah, my friend Dewey was telling me that five or six of the Mecklenburg wrestlers have ringworm. He doesn't know if they'll be able to wrestle us."

"Who's Dewey?" butted in Coach.

"We played baseball together last summer. He wrestles at Mecklenburg," Tyler answered. "He called me up last night about baseball sign-ups, and we started talking about wrestling."

"You play baseball, too?" asked Coach, looking surprised.

Tyler gave him a questioning look. "What? You don't think I can play two sports?"

"No, I just thought wrestling was your only sport," blinked Coach.

"Yeah, right," said Tyler, not fooled. "People are always pre-judging me about what I can or can't do, but I think I can do anything."

Coach cleared his throat, embarrassed. "Your baseball buddy was saying that some of the Mecklenburg boys have ringworm?"

"That's what he said."

"If they wrestled us, would we get the ringworms, too?" asked Travis. "We won't have worms coming out of our butts like dogs do when we go to the bathroom, will we?" He wasn't trying to be funny. He was worried.

"Uh, no, Travis, nothing that gross," explained Coach. "Actually, it's not even internal. It's more like a round fungus that shows up on the skin, but it's very contagious. Wrestlers need a doctor's clearance before they can wrestle again."

* * * * *

A strange thing happened when we went to Mecklenburg to weigh in for our match. Coach noticed that a number of the Mecklenburg boys were already wearing their uniforms as they nervously milled around Butcher and Lenny Langston. Others were wearing T-shirts. Something was up. Coach shook his head and looked over at the referee standing by the scales, Bubba Taylor. "These boys are supposed to be wearing only their underwear when they weigh in. Nothing else."

Butcher gave him a sneering look. "What is it with you, Waters? Gotta see the boys in their underwear?"

Jimmie Ray pointed his finger at Butcher. "The rules clearly state that wrestlers must be checked for skin infections," he said in an accusing tone. "I thought you knew everything, Mr. Butcher."

"Guess we better show the coach our underwear," smirked a Mecklenburg wrestler, removing his singlet. He sounded pretty nervous, though.

Another boy mumbled something under his breath as he removed his T-shirt. He narrowed his eyes and bit down on his lips. He had trouble written all over his face.

Coach stood next to Bubba Taylor and looked closely as each Mecklenburg boy stepped on the scales. He quickly scanned their chest and arms, then their backs. When their 90-pounder stepped up, Coach peered closely at the boy's chest.

"Getting an eye full, coach?" snickered an upper weight Mecklenburg wrestler.

Jimmie Ray moved quickly to where the comment came from. "Shut...your...mouth!" he said slowly and deliberately. He turned to Butcher. "You've got great control of your team, coach!"

Butcher tossed his head. "You coach your team, I'll coach mine!"

"Wait a second here, Bubba!" Coach cried, pointing to the boy's chest. "Take a look at this!"

Bubba took a closer look at the boy's chest. "What's on your skin, son?"

"I...I don't know what you're talking about!"

Bubba picked up a towel and rubbed at the boy's chest. "Pancake makeup!" he declared, exposing a ringworm the size of a quarter. "You're not wrestling with ringworm!"

Coach looked at Butcher and Lenny Langston and shook his head in disgust. Three other boys were found with pancake makeup trying to hide their ringworm. One boy had it in four different places on his body. All were disqualified.

14

We went back to the visitors' locker room with everyone buzzing. Coach was trying to quiet everyone down when Bubba Taylor opened the door. He motioned Coach Waters and Jimmie Ray outside. "First of all, Coach Butcher said he had no knowledge of the players trying to cover up their ringworm," he began.

Jimmie Ray brushed off the referee with a wave of his hand. "Don't insult us, Bubba! That's bullshit and you know it!"

Bubba ignored the comment. "This is a big deal for these kids to wrestle in front of their own school. Three of those boys are ninth graders," he tried to reason. "Coach Butcher offered to cover the ringworm with bandages and tape."

"What are you saying, Bubba?"

He cleared his throat. "If it's okay with you guys, I'll let them wrestle if everything is covered up. It's their last chance in front of their school."

Jimmie Ray gave an exasperated look. "Rules are rules, Bubba! If you let them wrestle, you'll be breaking the rules the same as the kids! No deal!" He turned and walked away.

Coach grinned at the ref. "You heard the man. No deal."

Harpers Ferry had already taken the floor and was loosening up on the mat when the Mecklenburg team emerged from the locker room. Their players glared at Coach Waters with contempt. The Mecklenburg principal, a short, balding man, grabbed a bullhorn and began walking back and forth in front of the stands. He quickly turned the gym into a circus-like atmosphere as he led the students in deafening cheers. The adrenaline was everywhere.

Chris Galford opened with a great match, only to get reversed and pinned in the final twenty seconds. The Lumberjacks followed it up with a quick pin over Ronnie Dillow, and though Stevie Reynolds won the next match, it was by a decision instead of a pin. It was a huge moral victory for Mecklenburg, holding a 12-3 lead. Only when Tyler Moore checked in at the scorer's table and went out alone on the mat did the gym suddenly become quiet.

"Wait a minute! What's going on here?" shouted the school principal, running out on the mat, bullhorn in hand. Coach and Jimmie Ray looked at each other, their eyebrows raised. The principal conferred with the referee, then went over to the bleachers to address the students.

"Now hear this, all you students of Mecklenburg Junior High!" he blared. "What we have here is a disgrace to our school! We have to forfeit a match to Harpers Ferry because we don't have anyone to fill this weight class!" Obviously he didn't know about the ringworm cover-up. "Look at their boy!" he droned on, eyeing Tyler. "We could easily have won this match!" Perhaps he didn't mean it the way it sounded, but that's the way he said it.

The crowd booed Tyler as the ref raised his arm in victory. After the principal had just put him down, and with the crowd booing him, Tyler would have been forgiven if he had gotten mad and flipped off the crowd. Not Tyler. He broke out into a huge smile. He began waving wildly to the crowd, then ran over to the surprised principal and used both arms to grab his hand and furiously started shaking it. The crowd stopped booing and began laughing, even cheering him. Tyler continued pumping the embarrassed principal's hand.

"You're crazy, Tyler!" we told him when he finally got back to the bench.

"Kindness kills!" he said with a smile, but we knew he had heard the principal's words.

The brief applause for Tyler came to a sudden halt when Travis Nutter scored a quick takedown on his opponent and rolled him over for a pin. We now had the lead and the fans began hissing and booing. But Mecklenburg came roaring back to take the next two matches, prompting the crowd to break out into their familiar Harpers Ferry chant. Tyler rose from his chair and began pacing in front of our team. "Listen to them!" he commanded. "They're singing that stupid little song again! *Mountain Brats and River Rats!* Dammit, I'm proud of who I am! Let's show those jokers some real Mountain Magic!" he shouted. "C'mon now! Mountain Magic!" You'd have thought he was a general leading his troops into battle.

It was perfect timing for another Mecklenburg forfeit, this one to Eddie Gilbert, who no one could beat anyhow. Out bounded Mecklenburg's self-appointed cheerleader, bullhorn in tow. Coach gave the referee a quizzical look, but Bubba simply rolled his eyes. "I cannot believe we are forfeiting another match to little Harpers Ferry!" shouted the principal, and you could feel his conviction. "We are more than four times their size and can't find someone to wrestle this boy? All you boys who weigh 116 pounds should be ashamed of yourselves for being in the stands instead of out here for your school!" He was dishing out the hurt, the shame and the poop all at once.

Fortunately for everyone in the gym, Mecklenburg didn't have to forfeit the other two matches where their wrestlers were disqualified. They had backups to wrestle those classes, though Matt Donaldson and Doug Sillex pinned them quickly. We won going away, 46-24. When our team lined up to shake hands with the Mecklenburg wrestlers, the Mecklenburg boys turned their backs on us and walked to their locker room.

15

The Harpers Ferry wrestling tournament, held at the county high school, signaled the end of the junior high school wrestling season in West Virginia. In the few short years it had been held, the competition made it perhaps the toughest tournament in the state along with the traditional Sherrard tournament. Independence and Sherrard were both coming, and Sherrard had a 29-1 record. A school that Harpers Ferry had never wrestled before, Cheat Lake, would also be there. They boasted a 26-3 record, but more importantly, or at least more intimidating, one of their wrestlers was the son of the West Virginia University head wrestling coach. And though Coach Waters didn't want to invite Mecklenburg, he was told in no uncertain terms that if Harpers Ferry expected to use the county's lone high school to host the event, then Mecklenburg damn well better be invited, too.

"This is a great idea," said Tyler, stepping on the scales in the locker room. "But how come everyone gets to weigh in the day before the tournament?"

"Because Coach Waters doesn't want any knuckleheads like you coming to the tournament and then not making weight," his father told him. "Some kids have to travel five or six hours and he wants to be sure everyone can wrestle. This is supposed to be a fun tournament, so everyone weighs in a day early. The coaches and principals verify the weight classes and fax it to us."

Tyler frowned. "But wouldn't it be easy for a team to cheat?"

* * * * *

Harpers Ferry opened the tournament against George Mason High School from Virginia, a school for grades seven through twelve. They had always had a wrestling team for the older boys, but this was their first year of mixing in the seventh and eighth graders. "Coach Waters, we've heard an awful lot of good things about your team," the George Mason coach said before the match. He was a young guy, probably in his first year of coaching, and he seemed in awe at the size of the tournament. "Most of our boys are really green, and I'd be grateful for any pointers your boys could offer. I know they'd like to learn from the best," he said as Coach beamed at the compliment.

"Everyone gather around," said Coach Waters after the Mason coach went back to his team. "This is Mason's first year of wrestling at this level, and their coach would appreciate any help you could give his boys. But do it in a nice way. No acting smug." Coach hated braggers almost as much as cheaters.

George Mason easily fell by a 73-9 score, but their boys were gracious in defeat and clearly looked up to our wrestlers. Tyler, continually improving throughout the season, wrestled a soft-spoken boy, pinning him in eighteen seconds. The boy gave Tyler a big grin. "You're a good wrestler," he said earnestly. "I didn't really expect to beat you."

After the teams had lined up for the traditional handshakes after the match, some of us went over and talked with the boys we had just stomped. "Now listen, Kyle," said Tyler after looking up his name on the score sheet. "The first thing you need to have is a positive attitude. I don't care how overmatched you think you are, you have to believe you can beat your guy if he makes a mistake. Just look for an opening and be ready if you see one."

Kyle narrowed his brown eyes and nodded, deep in thought. "Next," continued Tyler, feeling very important after getting the boy's full attention, "you stood too high when you faced me instead of crouching lower. You won't get many takedowns in that position." He demonstrated a few takedown shots on him in slow motion, telling him how to position his feet and keep his balance for defense. The boy was bubbly in his thanks and wrapped an arm around Tyler's neck. "Thanks for your help. Maybe it will help me win a few matches." Tyler beamed at the praise and walked away feeling like an expert.

Tyler was still smiling to himself as our team prepared to face Cheat Lake. "I just gave my last opponent a few pointers. It should help him win a few matches," he said nonchalantly, sitting down next to Danny.

The boys looked across the mat at the Cheat Lake team. Danny looked at Tyler with a sly grin, "Guess who you have to wrestle, Tyler?"

"Doesn't matter to me."

"Good," smiled Danny. "Because you have to wrestle the son of the head wrestling coach at West Virginia University. He's undefeated."

"You're kidding."

Danny yawned. "Look at the bright side, Tyler. Maybe *he'll* give *you* some pointers after the match."

Tyler stopped smiling. He felt stupid for telling Kyle to have a positive attitude no matter how overmatched you thought you were. Right.

Chris Galford started the match by quickly falling behind his much larger and more muscled Cheat Lake opponent. But he bided his time, and when the kid made a wrong move, you could see the adrenaline flowing as Chris flipped the big boy over his back for a pin. It was easy. Just the way Tyler had told Kyle.

After Ronnie lost a tough match and Stevie scored a pin, Tyler found out right away why his opponent was undefeated. He took Tyler down immediately. The oohs and aahs rippled through the stands as the boy twisted Tyler like a pretzel, then cranked him on his neck with Tyler's feet sticking straight up in the air. It was pretty humbling. As Tyler walked off the mat he saw Kyle give him a sad-looking smile. Danny, his best friend, was laughing so hard he literally fell over backwards in his chair.

Maybe Tyler's exhibition in futility loosened things up for our team. He sat on the bench, laughing, pretending to cover his head in feigned embarrassment. Everyone strolled over to jokingly give him high-fives. But we were practically unbeatable after that. We lost only one more match to Cheat Lake, then crushed our next three opponents to finish 5-0 on the day.

But it was the day's final match between Mecklenburg and Sherrard that had everyone talking.

Over and over the crowd roared, and everyone knew that Mecklenburg had to be scoring a major upset. The noise went on, one match after another, until Coach finally went over to the far end of the gym see what was happening. Mecklenburg had jumped out to a 36-12 lead, only to see Sherrard come storming back. As Coach watched the Sherrard comeback, something caught his attention. Something wasn't quite right and seemed out of place. So while Sherrard won six of the last seven matches to hand the Mecklenburg boys a stunning defeat, Coach struck up a conversation with a Mecklenburg reserve who had left the team to go buy a drink.

"Young man," Coach Waters said pleasantly, "who's that boy that's wrestling right now?"

The boy was happy to talk. "Oh, we really mixed up our lineup. That's..." He went on to eagerly point out a number of different changes in the lineup. Coach nodded quietly to what he was saying.

When the day's wrestling was completed, Coach stopped by the tournament director's table. He collected all the score sheets to take home and look over.

16

Both Sherrard and Harpers Ferry entered the tournament's second day of wrestling with 5-0 records. The gym was packed with contingents of parents milling together in the stands. Younger children amused themselves by running up and down the bleacher steps while wrestlers streamed in and out of the gym, feasting on snacks from the concession stand. It was good knowing we didn't have to worry about making weight for another year.

Our team jumped on Sherrard the way Mecklenburg had done the day before. When Eddie Gilbert scored a twelve-second pin, our lead looked comfortable at 31-18. A few people began shouting, "Bring that championship trophy home!" but the celebration was premature. Sherrard had a veteran team and knew how to fight back. Slowly they began chipping away at our lead. They never gave up. It was like sad old times for our team when Artie Badger went out in the last match and pinned his opponent, because the match had already become meaningless. Sherrard was the winner, 42-40. As our team lined up to shake hands after the match, everyone was thinking the same thing. Once more we had the championship in our grasp only to let it slip away.

We took out our frustration by ripping through our next three opponents, beating each of them by twenty-five points or more. Our final match was a showdown for second place against Mecklenburg.

"They're up to something," Coach Waters said to Jimmie Ray. He looked over at the Mecklenburg coaching staff. They were all huddled together at the far end of the bleachers. Butcher, Langston, Fazolli, and their token head coach. They kept looking over at our team.

"Probably trying to match up against us," shrugged Jimmie Ray.

"No, they're up to something." Coach Waters pulled the Mecklenburg roster out of his pocket and studied it carefully. "They got away with it yesterday, but it's not happening today."

"What's that, Mac?"

"You'll see, Jimmie Ray. You'll see."

Coach went over to the scorer's table and turned in his team lineup, then went back to his chair and stared at Butcher. He was waiting for Butcher to turn in his lineup, but Butcher never moved. Finally the scorekeeper called out, "The match is ready to begin. The 75-pound wrestlers need to check in."

Chris Galford and his Mecklenburg opponent both moved to the table, but Coach Waters intercepted them. "Hold on a second," he said to the scorekeeper. "Mecklenburg hasn't turned in their lineup yet."

Butcher rolled his eyes from the Mecklenburg bench and bellowed, "C'mon, Waters! Your lineup is the wrestler that checks in for each match!"

"This isn't a duals match where you can change your mind at the last moment," he said evenly. "Under tournament rules, you've got to submit your lineup at the beginning of the match with no substituting."

Butcher was walking across the mat towards the scorer's table. "You need to check the rules, coach. I can send up any wrestler I want for each match, just the same as you did last year."

A thin smile crossed Coach Water's face at the mention of last year's match when he had out-maneuvered Butcher. But this was a tournament match and the rules were different. "I'm telling you, the lineup must be turned in before the teams begin to wrestle," he said firmly. The scorekeeper, the mother of a boy wrestling on another team, shrugged her indifference at knowing the rule.

Butcher gave Coach a look like he was revolted. "Learn the rules, Waters!" he snipped. He turned to the ref. "We're ready to go!"

"Coach, what are we waiting for?" the young referee asked wearily.

Coach turned around to Jimmie Ray who was watching the conversation from the end of the bench. "Jimmie Ray, get over here with your damn rule book!"

Jimmie Ray made his way to the scorer's table and pulled out his ever-present rulebook. He presented an open book to the referee who looked a little uneasy. Finally he nodded his head and turned to Butcher. "Tournament rules state your lineup has to be turned in before the match starts, coach. No substitutions. The lineup you turn in is the lineup you wrestle with. You need to turn it in."

Butcher gave a look of contempt before going back to his coaches. They shook their heads, nodded, then looked over again at the Harpers Ferry wrestlers. Finally Butcher penciled in changes to his lineup. He returned to the scorer's table and, with brown, beady eyes that never left Coach's face, dropped his lineup on the table. It was showdown time.

17

B oth teams' benches and chairs faced each other from opposite sides of the gym, and behind them the bleachers were packed. "Let's get this match started!" yelled the referee.

Coach walked over to the scorer's table and began copying down the names of Mecklenburg's lineup. Chris Galford went out for the first match. If Coach saw anything out of the ordinary, he didn't tip it off. He just nodded and looked over at Butcher. The Mecklenburg coach stared him dead in the eye.

"This will be a great way to end the season if we can beat Mecklenburg and take second place," wheezed Tyler to Danny.

"You sure you're all right, Tyler?" asked Danny. "You don't sound so good."

Two nights earlier Tyler had a breathing attack when his lungs filled with mucus. Once again his father had to rush him to the hospital. He was kept overnight for monitoring and given drugs to clear up his lungs and help him sleep. When he awoke early the next morning he had a fit, demanding the nurses call his father to check him out of the hospital. It didn't matter that the doctor had recommended he not wrestle on Friday. He didn't *order* Tyler not to wrestle and, by golly, he was going to wrestle anyhow. Mr. Moore knew it would have been useless to argue with Tyler and had already been on his way to the hospital to pick him up.

At the tournament, Tyler had wrestled all day on Friday and done well, winning three of five matches. But that night in bed he had another relapse, though not nearly as bad as Thursday. He had done a good job of muffling his breathing from his mother, who would have laid down the law and kept him home on Saturday no matter what he or his father said.

"What difference does it make if I don't feel so hot?" Tyler said to Danny. "I've got to wrestle. The team needs me." He was really sucking in air after wrestling four more matches on Saturday. It had taken everything out of him. By the time it was his turn to wrestle again, Mecklenburg had quickly jumped out to a 9-3 lead.

"Do you think he can wrestle?" Coach asked Tyler's father standing next to him.

Big Bill looked over at his son. "He's not doing too well, but the little knucklehead would honestly try to kick my butt if I told him he couldn't wrestle."

"He's a helluva competitor."

"More stupidity than brains," replied Big Bill.

"Maybe just more courage than brains," suggested Coach.

Tyler put down a bottle of water he was drinking from and went on the mat with a determined look on his face. He knew he could take this boy. The referee blew his whistle and Tyler circled the mat, looking for an opening to take his opponent down. On and on the boys circled each other. Finally Tyler shot for his opponent's legs, but he was totally exhausted and his move lacked quickness. The boy blocked Tyler's lunge with his left arm, then spun to the right to get behind him and gain control. "Aaaggg!" screamed Tyler as the boy tightened his grip around his stomach. Tyler thrashed around the mat, using what little energy he had left. The buzzer sounded, ending the first period with the Mecklenburg wrestler out in front, 2-0. Tyler stood up holding his stomach, his mouth open and tongue out. "I...I need to get sick," he mumbled to the ref, still holding his stomach.

"Injury time out!" yelled the ref.

Big Bill hurried towards Tyler, but Tyler waved him off. He ran towards a trashcan at the other end of the gym. He leaned over the can and emptied his stomach, then ran back to the mat and looked at his father. "Don't even ask!" Tyler said loudly.

The other boy tossed Tyler around the mat. If Tyler was embarrassed he didn't show it. He had only one thing on his mind and that was not to be pinned. In the third period the referee again called an injury timeout when Tyler began getting dry heaves on the mat. He was soaking wet but refused to look at his father or the other coaches, instead waving them away as he gulped for air. In the stands his mother watched the scene unfold with a hand over her mouth.

"How much time is left?" Tyler asked.

The referee turned to look at the clock. "Twenty-two seconds. Are you sure you can continue?"

"Let's get it finished then." He wasn't going to give up a six-point forfeit.

The referee blew his whistle to resume the match. Tyler was on the bottom as the Mecklenburg boy desperately jerked him around the mat trying to pin him before the buzzer. Tyler's breaths came in short, wheezing gasps. He never gave up, even as the boy finally turned him on his back. Tyler closed his eyes and summoned all his remaining strength as he bridged his body off the mat to buy a few desperate seconds, but it wasn't enough. The referee's hand came down a moment before the buzzer sounded. He was pinned. The Mecklenburg wrestler released his grip on Tyler as his body lay crumpled on the mat. Tyler woozily got to his feet and shook his opponent's hand, then almost blindly stumbled toward the Mecklenburg bench to shake their coach's hand.

Tyler walked back to the Harpers Ferry bench and passed Travis going out for the next match. Travis reached out to shake his hand. "Any other time I could have taken him," insisted Tyler, stung with the thought that he had let his team down. His forced breathing wheezed from his body.

Travis went out on the mat and eyed his Mecklenburg opponent suspiciously, a boy named Rollins. He seemed awful familiar. He shook his head trying to remember. He knew he'd seen this kid wrestle before, but hadn't it been against Stevie earlier in the year? How'd the boy move up two weight classes?

Coach looked across the mat at Butcher, then leaned over and whispered something to Jimmie Ray. He started to rise from his seat, but before he stood up Travis had put the boy away and the match was over. After that the two teams seesawed back and forth. By the time we reached the 135-pound bout Mecklenburg maintained a 28-23 lead.

Evan Whalen checked in first at 135. When the boy from Mecklenburg checked in, Coach got up and walked over to the scorer's table. He peered down at the boy's name, then showed the scorer a roster of the Mecklenburg wrestlers. When the scorer shook her head and shrugged, Coach walked out on the mat. It was time to play his ace in the hole.

18

This was the young referee's very first tournament. He should never have been working such an important match. There was too much animosity between the two teams and too much pressure on every call. Yet strangely enough, the head referee of the six-man crew, Bubba Taylor, had assigned him to the biggest match of the tournament. It was like no one else wanted to do it. And no amount of training could have prepared the young referee for the bombshell that Coach dropped.

"This boy signed in under the name Jason Noonan, and he is not Jason Noonan!" Coach told him. "They're using an ineligible player!"

The young referee looked at Coach incredulously. "What are you trying to tell me?"

"That kid isn't who he says he is," answered Coach, pointing to the boy standing next to Evan Whalen. "He isn't Jason Noonan."

By now Butcher knew the jig was up but was determined to play out the charade. "Whaddaya holding up the match for, Waters?" he shouted from the other end of the mat. "Let the boys wrestle!"

"What do you want me to do?" asked the referee. He was pretty clueless.

"Dammit, they're cheating! They forfeit the match! There's nothing to think about!"

The referee was unconvinced. "If the boy signed in as Jason Noonan, then he must be Jason Noonan. Let's wrestle!" It never occurred to him that they really were cheating.

Butcher stood in front of the Mecklenburg bench next to Lenny Langston. He could clearly see Coach was having trouble convincing the referee, but he made no effort to join the meeting. "C'mon, Waters, get over it! Let the boys wrestle!" he shouted, inciting the crowd behind him. The Mecklenburg fans were a mean bunch and began chanting for the match to begin. Even their wrestlers joined in the heckling.

Coach stood his ground. Back and forth he went with the referee, insisting Mecklenburg was cheating. Then things got as nasty as you'll ever see at a public school sporting event. The Mecklenburg crowd began hurling insults at Coach, vilifying him with every evil name possible. Finally he crossed toward the Mecklenburg bench and yelled to Lenny Langston. "Tell the truth, Lenny! Dammit, tell the truth!"

Butcher reached over and put a restraining hand on Langston's shoulder, staring straight ahead. Coach began to flounder. Lenny Langston didn't move a muscle to help his former coach as the referee tried to regain control of the match. "Get your boy back out there to wrestle, coach, or you forfeit the match!"

"Like hell I will!" shot back Coach. By now even the Harpers Ferry fans were getting restless. Some began grumbling to get on with the match. Even our players wondered what he was doing. We began turning to each other, confused, shrugging our shoulders. He was a man alone.

The sneer on Butcher's face was a mile wide. He had Coach and he knew it. The booing reached a crescendo as the Mecklenburg crowd rained their venom on Coach Waters. Even the Harpers Ferry fans openly began calling to wrestle. Coach was bathed in perspiration. Evan and the Mecklenburg boy edged back into the center of the mat. "I'm starting the match now, coach. Get off the mat. Get off the mat or I'm calling a forfeit!" he declared.

Coach was beaten. All the wrestling in the gym had come to a halt as coaches and players from other teams crowded around the mat. The drama was intense. Coach looked back at the jeering Mecklenburg crowd. No one knew what was happening. Even his own players didn't know whether to be ashamed of him or just feel sorry for him. He was a tired, beaten man as he walked off the mat to the storm of insults. What happened next brought the gym down. Just as he got to the bench, Coach suddenly whirled around and shouted above the crowd, "ASK THAT BOY HIS NAME!"

The referee leaned over the boy, and the boy quietly said, "Henry Mueller." The referee threw up his hands. "Ineligible wrestler! Mecklenburg forfeits to Harpers Ferry!" Mecklenburg had cheated!

"The whole match is over, right, ref?" Coach asked. "Any sport, you use an ineligible player, you forfeit the game!"

Butcher came running over, showing no remorse for his cheating. "Now look here, ref, if you call the whole match, it's going to affect the outcome of the wrestlers' individual standings. The top three wrestlers in each weight class get a trophy. You can't just throw out the rest of the matches. It's not fair to our kids who have a chance to win a trophy." He was petty brash.

Coach looked at Butcher like the man had gone mad. No apology for cheating, no explanation, no nothing. Just carry on like it was a beautiful day. The 135-pound forfeit pulled our team ahead, 29-28, with four matches left. No one was going to beat Doug Sillex or Artie Badger. All we had to do was win at either 145 pounds or 165 pounds and that would do it. But our 145-pounder got pinned, and while Doug had already pinned his opponent twice during the season, he couldn't put him away this time. He got three points for a decision instead of six for pinning. Mecklenburg remained in front, 34-32. Still, if our 165-pounder didn't get pinned and Artie got one himself, as he had done over thirty times already during the season, the match belonged to Harpers Ferry.

For the Harpers Ferry wrestlers, however, it was like seeing our life flash before our eyes a second time. It was the Sherrard match all over again. Wrestling is a tough sport and not everyone can handle the pressure. Maybe our 165-pounder just wasn't meant to be a wrestler. He went out to the mat and froze on the whistle, standing up instead of crouching down. The Mecklenburg boy made the pin look easy.

It was over. Butcher looked across the gym and met Coach's eyes. A superior look was on his face. Everyone watched in a daze as Artie went out and scored a pin in the last match, but it didn't matter. We had finished in third place with an 8-2 record.

Our season had ended with a 30-7 mark, but what really hurt was losing two tournaments in almost identical fashion to the same two teams. And Mecklenburg had cheated and gotten away with it! Our players sat in stony silence as the Mecklenburg boys went smugging themselves around the gym. They were slapping high-fives to everyone in sight like they were God's gift to the wrestling world.

There was a light tap on Tyler's shoulders. It was Kyle. "Sorry you guys lost. I was rooting for you," he said sadly, adding, "I think everyone was." He held a black sweatshirt in his hand and looked down at it. "Our coach gave everyone a George Mason sweatshirt to give to someone," he said. "Someone who helped us become a better wrestler." He cleared his throat and looked at Tyler. "He said to give it to someone we admired. This is for you."

Tyler didn't know what to say. He felt surprised and a little embarrassed until he looked around and saw that Travis, Stevie and Artie were also receiving sweatshirts. "Gosh, Kyle," he gulped. "You guys are really a class act."

"No, Tyler, you guys are. Especially you."

Tyler nodded thankfully and shook hands with Kyle. Tyler turned and walked away, almost feeling a little bit better. Then he saw Ronnie Dillow sitting by himself. Ronnie was trying to choke back the soft sounds from his throat by burying his dark hair in his hands. "Dammit! Dammit! Dammit!" he repeated to himself. He looked up with puffy eyes when Tyler walked by and said, "They can't do that and get away with it! It's not fair! Cheaters aren't supposed to win!"

Tyler looked at Ronnie and put his hand on his shoulder. "My dad always told me there are a lot of things in life that aren't fair, Ronnie. It doesn't matter how or why things happen to you, you just gotta deal with it." He shook his head almost in acceptance. "I stopped questioning things a long time ago. Yeah, we got cheated today. But it's not the end of the world. Dad tells me that when you get cheated you have to try harder and become a better person because of it. I know I am. You just have to believe that good things are going to happen to you." He walked away from Ronnie and pressed his thumb and forefinger against his eyes. The team would have won today if he hadn't been pinned.

Coach knew Tyler was unnecessarily blaming himself and went to console him. He was turning out to be a powerful inspiration for our team.

"Mac, that was tough!" commented Sherrard coach Ralph Barnett, coming up behind Coach. "They were cheating, weren't they?" He knew. "You call me in a few days and let me know all the details. I know you don't want to talk about it now."

Coach shook his head resolutely. "Yeah, it was tough. But I'm glad it was you who won the tournament. You've had a helluva season."

Coach Barnett laughed. "Yeah, we finished 39-1. How sweet it would've been to go undefeated at 40-0. No team has ever won forty games or matches in a single season in any West Virginia sport." He rolled his eyes to where Butcher, Lenny Langston, and the token head coach were accepting congratulations and slapping butt cheeks on everyone. "You can be damn sure I'll do my best to keep those bums from ever getting invited to another tournament!"

Maybe that provided the spark for the fire that kindled next. "Hey, coach! Got a minute?" called out a reporter for the local newspaper. It was often referred to as *The Urinal* because of the number of inaccuracies in its reporting. "I saw you and the ref in that big hullabaloo during the Mecklenburg match. Have any comment on what was going on?"

"Yeah, I've got quite a few comments. Like Mecklenburg was cheating! Entering kids under false names and different weight classes! You want a story? I'll give you a story!"

Jimmie Ray put an arm out. "Don't talk to him now, Mac," he cautioned. "Wait till you cool off. You need to think about what you're going to say"

"What's to think about?" demanded Coach, pulling away from Jimmie Ray. "They cheated us and other schools, and they're not going to get away with it! I'm filing a grievance with the State Athletic Commission!" He turned to the reporter. "You want a story? Let's go!"

19

A light snow had fallen during the night on Blue Ridge Mountain. The swirling wind was spinning the snow around in circles as Tyler walked down the long dirt lane of his driveway to retrieve the morning newspaper. He coughed, pulling his undershirt up around his neck to keep warm. The pain of losing to Mecklenburg came back to him in waves of remorse, and when he stooped to pick up the paper, he saw immediately that the newspaper had not been kind to Coach Waters.

In the upper right hand corner of the front page, where the paper always carried a small picture and caption of a sporting event, was a snippet showing two boys wrestling. Under the picture was, *"Controversy Surrounds Harpers Ferry Wrestling Tourney."* Tyler flipped to the sports section. Beneath the enlarged photo from the front page was the screaming headline:

HARPERS FERRY FINISHES THIRD;
COACH SAYS TEAM CHEATED
Formal complaint to be filed
with State Athletic Commission by losing coach.

Tyler quickly scanned the article as he walked back to the house. It detailed how Coach Waters had gotten into a heated argument with a Mecklenburg coach over the rules and procedures of their match. How it later exploded into accusations of cheating.

The newspaper wrote that Coach Waters reportedly said that Mecklenburg had illegally wrestled boys out of their weight classes against several teams on Friday. He also said they used a backup wrestler certified at 123 pounds to accept a forfeit at the 116-pound weight class against George Mason. Waters went on to claim that against Harpers Ferry, Mecklenburg had illegally moved one wrestler up four weight classes. The boy, Henry Mueller, had been instructed by Butcher to wrestler under a false name. Earlier in the same match, Mecklenburg had illegally moved a boy, LaMont Rollins, up two weight classes from 85 pounds to 95 pounds.

"This is the most blatant cheating I have ever seen!" Coach Mac Waters had insisted. "Those boys knew they were cheating when they went out on the mat, and they did so because Dick Butcher told them to do it! Their team is a disgrace!"

Tyler read the entire article. "Wow! Coach Waters didn't mince any words," he mumbled. There was a queasiness in his stomach. He wondered if maybe Coach or the newspaper had gone too far. When he got back to the house his father was on the phone with Coach Waters.

At lunchtime Danny and Travis stopped by Tyler's house. "You guys aren't going to believe what's going on!" Tyler greeted them breathlessly. "Coach could really be in a lot of trouble!"

"We read the article," Danny said. Travis nodded with raised eyebrows. His face was full of questions.

"Coach Waters told my dad he was at McDonald's this morning when he ran into a guy from the school board office. He really laid Coach out!" continued Tyler. "Said he had given the school system a black eye that it may never recover from!"

"But why?" Travis wanted to know. "For telling the truth? They *were* cheating for chrissakes!"

"That doesn't matter," Tyler informed them. "He told Coach he should've kept quiet and not put his dirty laundry out in the newspaper. Said Mr. Butcher and Henry Mueller's father were threatening to sue the school board. They want him fired!"

"Who is this guy?"

"His name is Roscoe Belcher. He's the guy from the board office who comes by our school with his hair in a ponytail to try and look cool. He's a real piece of work," said Tyler with a laugh. "But Coach said he's a real bully of a person. The guy's on a major power trip and thinks he runs the whole show at the board office," Tyler went on. "All the teachers in the county say he either likes you or hates you. There's no in-between."

"What's going to happen to Coach?"

"I don't know," answered Tyler. "But Dad said Coach is plenty worried. This Belcher guy can be a vindictive person and carries a lot of grudges. Now the old bully has Coach right in his crosshairs!"

"Do you think Coach is going to get fired?" asked Travis hesitantly.

"Let's put it this way," suggested Tyler with a deep sigh. "My dad told Coach to get himself a *really damn good lawyer.*"

* * * * *

There is an old adage that *"Cheaters never win."* That's not always true, as our team found out. Cheaters do win, and it doesn't necessarily have to be in the final score. They can beat you the way Mecklenburg cheated us and the other schools, or they can beat you in other ways. The Mecklenburg wrestling team had been embarrassed, and so had our county school system, about the allegations of cheating. In this case it was simply better to pretend that it had never happened.

Whenever people in the county talked about the *"tournament fiasco,"* and many people did, it was always with a very one-sided view. If you listened to people talk outside of the Harpers Ferry community, you would never have known that Mecklenburg had cheated. It was Coach Waters who was hell-bent on disgracing the good students at Mecklenburg Junior High. He was a sore loser who couldn't handle defeat. He was the one who was setting a poor example and should be fired. What was wrong with letting a boy wrestle?

There was no sympathy from the school board office. The newspaper article had been picked up and reprinted in practically every newspaper in the state. Our county cheated in sports. This was not good. It didn't matter that the county would have been liable for negligence and medical costs if one of the underweight boys had been injured. A broken bone or spinal injury, no matter whose fault, could have cost the county millions of dollars in a lawsuit. But this did not happen and so was not considered. No, Coach Waters should have kept his big mouth shut. Everything should have been kept in the family.

Coach Waters, despite a warning from the board office, did file a grievance with the State Athletic Commission. The incident was fully investigated, and Mecklenburg was hit with a one-year probation for "flagrant" cheating. It came with the promise that another violation would result in the revocation of their program. But this was not really detrimental to Mecklenburg. The probation was quietly swept under the table and not made public. If you looked at everything from face value, Coach Waters was the guilty person. A troublemaker.

Roscoe Belcher saw to it that the county wrote a letter of apology to Henry Mueller's father. Coach Waters was ordered down to the board office to sign the letter. "You will sign this document, Mr. Waters," said Roscoe Belcher, placing the letter in front of Coach with a coldness that raised the hair on his arms.

"What is it?"

"You are acknowledging total responsibility for the boy's name appearing in the newspaper." Belcher's face was taut and expressionless. "It will exonerate the county for your loose lips should the boy's father decide to sue."

"And if I don't sign it?"

"You can start looking for another job. Today." Belcher smiled at Coach with calculating eyes.

Roscoe Belcher was not yet finished. To make sure that Coach Waters fully understood that he alone was responsible for the mess in the newspaper, he went to see our principal, Mr.

Crawford. He directed him to write a formal letter of reprimand that was to be placed in Coach Waters' personnel file. When Coach was called into Mr. Crawford's office to sign the letter, Belcher told him with absolute authority, "You are unfit to be a teacher, Mr. Waters. You are a disgrace to the profession."

"How would you know? You've never seen me teach! You've never seen me coach!"

"I know all I want to know about you, Mr. Waters," he said in a dismissing tone.

The message was clear. You don't blow whistles about sports in our county.

* * * * *

Our wrestling team held its annual end-of-the-year cookout on the last Thursday in May. The banquet was followed with an awards presentation where the coaches took turns telling stories and anecdotes about each of the wrestlers. Everyone got a big trophy, no matter how good or how bad we were.

When it came time to give Tyler his trophy, Coach Waters frowned as he leaned into the microphone. "I'm ashamed to say that when this next young man first came out for the team two years ago, I didn't think he would make it. I didn't think he was tough enough. I thought there might be too many things holding him back," he said, trying to pick his words carefully. Everyone knew then who he was talking about. "But there are some things you can't measure, at least not with this boy. And I'm talking about the size of his heart. Tyler Moore."

The crowd began clapping. After Tyler went on stage to receive his trophy, he turned and reached his hand out to the audience. His forefinger and thumb were nearly touching, indicating his heart was too small to measure. Everyone went wild and broke out laughing and cheering. Coach could only shake his head. The smile on his face was a mile wide.

When the banquet was drawing to a close, Coach concluded by saying, "I want to thank all the boys and parents for making this such a successful season. And for the boys coming back next year, I honestly think we will have *a once-in-a-lifetime team.*"

Tyler Moore sat in the crowd and nodded carefully to Coach Waters' words. "If I have anything to do with it, next season will be something that people will talk about forever," he agreed silently to himself. "It *will* be a season to remember."

Part Three
<u>Ninth Grade</u>
20

N one of us could for wait for wrestling season to start the following school year. It's all we ever talked about, even in September. One morning we were all sitting around a cafeteria table eating breakfast when we had one of our usual spirited discussions about the upcoming season. "With practically our whole team back, I think we'll do even better than last year," spoke up Evan Whalen.

"It'll be hard to top thirty wins again," commented Danny. "You can't get much better than that."

"We should have won more than thirty matches last year," Travis argued. "We lost some matches we could have won."

"That won't happen this year," agreed Tyler. "We need to really stay focused and concentrate on every match. There's no telling what we can accomplish if no one screws around."

"And what do you think we'll accomplish?" I asked jokingly.

Tyler didn't laugh. He was dead serious. "I've been thinking about our team all summer. I read an article about how all the junior highs in the state are going to become middle schools over the next two years. That means a lot of changes in the sports programs. Fewer games. Less travel. No overnight trips."

"So?" shrugged Stevie Reynolds. "It won't affect us. We'll be in high school next year."

"Don't you see? We're ninth graders," Tyler said with a shake of his head. "We *are* in high school."

Chris Galford looked around the cafeteria. "This looks like a junior high school to me," he smirked. Everything was a big joke to the *Little Beast* except wrestling.

"Don't you guys get it?" asked Tyler in exasperation. "In junior high schools we have ninth graders, so we're considered a secondary school. Same as the high schools."

"And?" Artie Badger joined in the conversation.

"Get to the point, Tyler," said Matt Donaldson. He was always so serious.

"Any records set by junior high schools are considered state secondary school records," explained Tyler. "We may just do something that's never been done before in West Virginia. We could go down in history," he added, nodding knowingly to us. "Trust me."

We all gave Tyler a puzzled look. Sometimes it was hard to figure out what was going through his head. But we knew one thing by his expression. He wasn't kidding around. Like most kids, Tyler had always thought it would be nice to set some kind of record, to do something that had never been done before. Even if the record was eventually broken, it would be nice to say that at one time you held the record. But it would be even sweeter to set a record that you *knew* would *never* be broken. And that's exactly what Tyler had in mind.

"It's now or never," thought Tyler as he turned the handle on Coach Waters door later that day. Coach had already packed up his grade book after the final bell and was heading for the door when Tyler breezed into his room. "Hi, Coach," he greeted. "Got a few minutes?"

"Sure, Tyler, what's on your mind?" he smiled. Coach never knew what to expect from him. None of us did.

Tyler made himself comfortable at a desk. "How would you like our wrestling team to do something that's never been done before? How would you like our team to be the only team in West Virginia history to win forty games or matches in a single season, in any sport?" He paused. "It would be something that we could carry with us for the rest of our lives."

Coach laughed, but it was an interesting thought. "How do you know that no team has ever won forty games before?"

"Because I remember the Sherrard coach telling you he wanted his team to be the first to do that. Anyhow, you could look it up." Tyler gave an innocent smile. "I did."

Coach put his hand to his chin. He was definitely thinking about it. "It would take a heckuva team to win forty matches. Figure we'd lose a few, and with other matches getting snowed out, I'd have to schedule forty-five or fifty matches just to have a chance. Why, it would be nothing short of a miracle to accomplish."

"We were 30-7 last season. With a little luck could have won all the matches. Sherrard had forty matches, and there's no reason we can't have that many and even a few more," Tyler reminded him. "You even said at the banquet we could have a once-in-a-lifetime team this year with practically everyone back. Even if we had to travel every weekend, it could be done. You could at least try and schedule the extra matches." Tyler was making a strong case.

"I don't know, Tyler," Coach said, rubbing his chin. "The snow. The traveling."

"Wrestling is the only sport left where a team has a chance to get forty games or matches in a season. High schools don't have a lot of dual matches because they wrestle mostly in bracket tournaments. When the junior highs become middle schools, everything will be cut down. If we won forty matches this year, no team would even have a chance to beat our record." Tyler narrowed his eyes the way he often did when he became serious. "There will never be an opportunity like this again. As my father always tells me, a person will never know what he can accomplish if he doesn't at least try."

Tyler was humming to himself when he left Coach Water's room. He had planted the seed and knew that something would grow from it.

21

"I'll resign before I wrestle Mecklenburg again!" Coach Waters said emphatically to his principal.

Mr. Crawford raised his eyebrows and gave Coach a tired look. "You don't seem to understand, Mr. Waters. We HAVE to wrestle Mecklenburg! It's not our choice. We can't just decide we don't want to play our county rival."

"Fine then. Get a new coach."

Mr. Crawford removed his glasses and looked across his desk. It was always cluttered with papers piled into stacks of varying sizes. He could never seem to find anything. "Mac, I don't understand your reasoning."

"Mecklenburg blatantly cheated us last year and their coaches are still allowed to coach. They get a little slap on the wrist. I have to sign a letter saying I was totally to blame for what happened. Then *YOU* put a damn letter of reprimand in my personnel file. And you don't understand my reasoning?" He glared back at the principal.

Mr. Crawford ignored Coach Waters' last comment. "We wrestle each other in front of our schools because our athletic departments need the money. It's always a sell-out crowd. The money pays for a lot of sports in a lot of ways. Roscoe Belcher at the school board office isn't going to let us dictate who we wrestle and who we don't. There's too much money at stake."

Coach Waters stood up. "I don't give a damn about your money. Either we drop Mecklenburg from our schedule or I quit. You can't force me to coach." He turned and walked out the office.

For the next two weeks our school was full of rumors. The only thing certain was that Mac Waters and Jimmie Ray Lawson would resign if Harpers Ferry was forced to wrestle Mecklenburg.

"But why are you quitting?" Tyler asked Coach one day during lunch. "You know we can beat Mecklenburg."

Coach looked around the cafeteria where our team had practiced the last six winters. Each year the cinderblock walls and the large, open windows on the far side had slowly yielded to darkness as the days of winter grew longer. "It's not about winning or losing. It's about integrity and doing what's right. It's about having principles and being accountable for what you do. I know you're too young to understand that now, but maybe one day you will. If we have to quit to get our point across, it will hurt me and Jimmie Ray a lot more than you'll ever know."

Big Bill Moore understood the coaches' dilemma. More than anything else, he wanted to watch and help coach his only son in his final season of wrestling at Harpers Ferry. He knew Tyler's chances of wrestling at the high school level would be minimal. This would be a season where Tyler could perhaps have a breakout year, and on paper our team looked powerful. But hadn't he also spent many years trying to teach Tyler about values and standing up for what you believed was right? That you had to believe in yourself and your own basic principles to be successful in life? That without self-character you were really only a shell of a person?

When it became apparent to Mr. Crawford that Coach Waters and Jimmie Ray Lawson would resign rather than wrestle Mecklenburg, he knew he had to reach some sort of compromise. There was too much money at stake and too many boys involved. It would also be a major embarrassment to him if his coaches quit. A call was made to the principal of Mecklenburg Junior High followed by a call to the board office. Two days later a meeting was held in our library at Harpers Ferry. Both the Mecklenburg principal, the rah-rah cheerleader from last year, and their athletic director, Boss Parker, were at the meeting. Roscoe Belcher came from the school board office. Mr. Crawford and Mr. Duval were there to represent Harpers Ferry with Coach Waters and Jimmie Ray. The men stared at each other across a long table in the center of the room surrounded by mountains of books.

Mr. Crawford began the meeting. "Gentlemen, I think we all know why we are here," he said with clasped hands.

"Mr. Waters," began the Mecklenburg principal. "The matches between our schools are a major fund raiser for both of us. That's why we have them during school hours, so the students can attend."

Roscoe Belcher glared at Coach Waters. "We can't have our schools pick and choose who they play and don't play in our own county. Frankly, you're acting like an elementary-age child with your demands." He wasn't happy.

"See here, Waters," said Boss Parker. "I don't understand why you have a problem. Our head wrestling coach from last year has already turned in his resignation. He's out of the picture. What exactly is it that would make you happy?" he said in exasperation.

Coach Waters looked straight at the athletic director without flinching. "Butcher and Langston were the ones responsible for cheating. I want them out of coaching. Today, tomorrow, forever. I don't want them ever coaching at Mecklenburg Junior High again."

A stillness dropped over the room with the eyes of every man darting from one person to another. Only Belcher's eyes did not move. He stared at Coach Waters, his facial expression unmoving and calloused.

Mr. Crawford spoke up, "I think that's a reasonable request. After all, what are we teaching our kids when adults cheat?"

"I already told Lenny Langston he was welcome back as an assistant coach. I'm not going to tell him now that he can't coach," Boss Parker said between clipped words. No one told Boss Parker what he could and couldn't do.

Coach Waters shook his head at Jimmie Ray. "I think we're wasting our time." He looked over in annoyance when someone at a nearby table began to loudly ruffle a newspaper, the person's face hidden behind the outstretched newsprint. The sound of the library clock seemed to tick louder.

"I think we can go along with Mr. Waters' request," agreed the Mecklenburg principal. After all, there was too much money at stake not to wrestle.

"So I have your word," Coach asked pointedly, his eyes fixed on Boss Parker, "that Dick Butcher and Lenny Langston will *never* coach at Mecklenburg again?"

"Yes." Boss Parker glared over at the Mecklenburg principal and Roscoe Belcher. He hadn't expected this.

"One more thing," said Coach Waters with raised eyebrows. We're planning on having another wrestling tournament to close out the season," he stated. "Mecklenburg won't be invited."

"See here, Waters, this whole meeting has been about building better relations between our schools," objected Parker. "That would be a slap in our face, not inviting a county school to a local tournament."

"That was a slap in our face when your team cheated at our tournament last year," replied Coach evenly. "Do you really think the schools that came last year will come again with Mecklenburg in it?" he asked incredulously. "They'll laugh in my face and there won't even be a tournament!"

Mr. Duval must have been thinking about the two thousand dollars Coach had turned over to the athletic department from the tournament last year. "Mr. Waters does have a point. We'll wrestle each other home and away during the season, but Mecklenburg won't be invited to our tournament. If all goes well, they'll be invited back the following year," he concluded.

"I think we all did a little compromising today," added Mr. Crawford. "I think the one-year suspension is fair." He had never liked Mecklenburg. The school got everything it wanted from the board office while he always had to grovel for textbooks and needed repairs. "Are we all in agreement?"

The other principal nodded. "I'm glad we can finally put this behind us."

Boss Parker folded his arms across his chest. He was used to getting his own way and didn't like Coach Waters one little bit. He wasn't like Ben Duval, who was a good guy and never complained when you ran up the score on his boys.

The newspaper reader slapped the paper shut with a loud pop. Tyler Moore rose from the table, nodding his approval as he gave Coach Waters a thumbs up. Coach rolled his eyes at the sight of Tyler. He should have known.

22

There was a strange excitement in the air that fall that hadn't come to the halls of our school in nearly thirty years. You could feel it. You could taste it. Boys walked with a confidence that would have been unthinkable in years past. Not overconfidence, but certainly a swagger. It was a persistent, growing feeling that our school was on the verge of something wonderful, something great. Like an impossible challenge that was going to be met head on.

By early November, with the beginning of the winter sports seasons only weeks away, basketball was almost an afterthought. All everyone wanted to talk about was wrestling. Even those students who had never seen a wrestling match were caught up in the fever. The scare that Coach Waters and Jimmie Ray wouldn't coach had been resolved. They had stood like righteous crusaders as they defended our school's honor and brought down the entire coaching staff of Mecklenburg Junior High. The message was clear. Mess with Harpers Ferry and be crushed.

But it was the speculation generated by a boy who still weighed less than 100 pounds that carried the pulse of our school. That boy was walking down the hallway with Danny, Travis and me when some girls pointed to us. "Tyler, is it true that the wrestling team is going to set an all-time state record that will never be broken?" gushed a seventh grade girl, stopping to stare at him from three feet away like he was off limits.

Tyler nodded importantly. His big green eyes perused the girl with interest the way a stallion might look over a young filly. "Our team has the horses or, as Coach likes to say, we've got the thoroughbreds to go all the way." Coach Waters had never said this, but it certainly sounded good.

"Good luck, Tyler," she said bashfully. "I heard you're pretty good." She gave him a smile that brought a rich pink hue to his cheeks. There was a stirring inside him. The girls walked away giggling, with the one girl looking back over her shoulder. She was smiling at Tyler.

"What have you been feeding those girls?" I asked.

"The same thing he's been feeding the whole school," answered Travis. He had shot up over the summer and was nearly six feet tall and looked even more like a string bean. "Tyler thinks we're going to be the first team to ever win forty games or matches in a single season. That we'll all go down in history." Travis shook his head as he looked over at Tyler.

"It's going to happen. Some way, somehow, it is going to happen," he promised.

"Does Coach even have forty matches scheduled this year?" wondered Danny.

"He will," Tyler said solemnly. He was a strong believer in faith. The fact that Coach Waters had never actually promised him he would schedule forty or more matches did not bother Tyler. He simply *knew that Coach would do it.*

"Tyler, it would take one miracle after another for your dream to come true. Finding enough tournaments to wrestle in is just the beginning," Travis told him. "What about the travel? It would mean four, five or six-hour trips over endless mountains, one way, almost every weekend. Having enough parents willing to drop everything and drive us week after week. It can't be done."

And finally, there was one thing that none of us would talk about because we knew it was something beyond our control. The brutal West Virginia winters. Snowstorms can come fast and unmercifully without warning, sweeping down from the high mountains deep into the valleys with blizzard-like ferocity, canceling schools for days or even a week or more at a time. No, it would take nothing short of a miracle to get forty matches in. Yet Tyler never wavered in his belief that his dream could be accomplished.

"You have to believe. You have to believe," he told us over and over again.

If there was one more necessary ingredient for our team's success, it was a sense of unity, and that was the one thing our team didn't lack. We had grown much closer since last year, hanging out together and becoming real friends. There's a big difference between being teammates with someone and being friends. Many of us had been on different youth league teams where everyone got along and pulled for the team, but when the game was over we invariably went our own ways. We liked each other, of course, but we weren't really friends.

That wasn't the case with our team. We had started doing everything together, like fishing or camping, going to the mall, things friends did. And even though we knew we might be fighting each other for a starting job when practice started, it didn't matter. Once you become friends with someone, you pull for them the way you'd want them pulling for you. And we did that, especially the eighth and ninth graders. We had already learned to stand up for each other the way our coaches had stood up for us against the Mecklenburg coaches.

After the first week of practice, the coaches led us to the locker room. "You boys are going to have to make a tough decision today, and it needs to be the right decision," said Jimmie Ray. "The coaches want you to select a team captain. We've never had a captain before, but we think this season's team is going to be special. He has to be someone you can look up to, someone who is going to be a role model for the whole team."

The coaches walked toward the door. Coach Waters turned and looked at us. "Think about it. Make a good choice."

When the coaches had left, Evan Whalen spoke up. "How about Stevie Reynolds? He's probably our best wrestler."

Stevie squirmed on the bench. "That's not really for me. I'd rather someone else was captain."

"How about Artie Badger? He's a great wrestler," said Mike "Smitty" Smith.

Artie shook his head. "I just go out and wrestle. We've got other guys who can crack the whip better than me. It's not about who's the best wrestler on our team."

Chris Galford spoke up. "Then how about Tyler? He ain't one of our best wrestlers. He qualifies. He's always jumping on us for doing something wrong." The *Little Beast* could really say dumb things. We loved him.

Everyone laughed. But everyone also nodded approvingly at Tyler. Certainly not our best wrestler, but no one cared more about our team than he did. That was a given.

"I nominate Tyler Moore for our team captain," said Doug Sillex. He broke into a wide grin. "He has big dreams for our team this year. Who knows, maybe some of them will come true. At least he cares."

We laughed again, but it was a friendly laugh. I voiced my opinion, "Tyler Moore for team captain."

Our hands went up. "Tyler for team captain."

Tyler pulled his head down and looked at his chest. He was embarrassed, but we knew he was proud. We also knew we had elected the one guy who could, *and would*, lead our team. Whether he was our best wrestler or not.

We didn't know it then, but our ride was just beginning.

23

Coach Waters had everything in place before the season started. Big Bill Moore would be back to help him and Jimmie Ray. Roland Proctor, a former Harpers Ferry wrestler, had also been approved by the school board to serve as a volunteer coach. Coach had put together a schedule that was arguably the toughest in the state. Forty-five matches with very few pushovers. We still had to wrestle Mecklenburg twice in dual matches, but Coach had used his other allotted matches to squeeze in six tournaments in six different regions of the state. Five of the tournaments would be overnight trips.

"We'll never be able to travel three thousand miles over the mountains and get all the overnight trips in. The snow will stop us," warned Jimmie Ray. "And if it doesn't, we'll be exhausted and going crazy by the end of the season with so much travel."

"I want to get forty-five matches in," Coach answered. "We might lose a few, but it won't be many. As someone once told me, there will never be an opportunity like this again."

Even without the graduated Eddie Gilbert, our team's line-up was truly powerful. We had a lot of familiar faces but in different weight classes, along with some unproven newcomers. Lovable Chris Galford, who still looked like a little blond-haired, ten-year-old kid that the women at all the tournaments loved to hug, was back for his third year at 75. He still only weighed 68 pounds. David Carter, an eighth grader who had only minimal success on the junior varsity team, was at 80; Ronnie Dillow, dark-haired, dark-eyed, and terribly bashful, had been bumped up to 85. Jake Patton, a second-year wrestler who always managed to drive Coach Waters up the wall with his complaining or excuses, weighed in at 90. Tyler, who had picked up a few pounds in the last year, was back at 95. Stevie Reynolds, still with a face full of freckles and shocking red hair, was at 102 as he closed in on the state junior high record for most career wins. Danny Schneider had beaten out a friend in Tommy Johnson for the 110 spot, while Ricky Stillson, a hot-tempered boy, was at 116. Travis, skinny as a pencil with a big goofy grin, was at 123. Following Travis was Mike Thomas at 128, our team's lone Afro-American wrestler and one of the school's best athletes who had shocked Ben Duval a year earlier by shunning basketball and becoming a star in his own right in wrestling.

After Mike came our team's strongest, toughest kids who refused to be intimidated by anyone. All of them were like a rock of granite. Coach fondly called them the *"Big Guns."* Matt Donaldson, with his serious personality and high standards, was at 135. Next came Evan Whalen, a role model of self-discipline, at 145. Doug Sillex, with his loose personality and awesome physical strength, was at 155. At 165 there were both Mike "Smitty" Smith and Dennis Wilson, close friends who wrestled each other every day in practice but who always pulled for each other. At heavyweight, of course, was Artie Badger, weighing only 175 pounds, but who never flinched about wrestling someone twice his size.

* * * * *

What started out as a season with high expectations almost got railroaded before it even began. With the opening tournament only two days away, a rapid-fire series of events suddenly unhinged our team. Chris Galford was caught smoking a cigarette on school property and was promptly suspended for three days. Two hours later, Danny Schneider received an incomplete grade on his report card, making him ineligible for any sports until it was changed to a letter grade. But the real icing came at the end of practice that day, long after most of the team had gone to the locker room to change clothes. Tyler and I and a few other boys were helping put away the mats in the cafeteria when Coach heard some moaning coming from a nearby bathroom.

Coach went to the bathroom and found a boy leaning over a sink, blood all over the floor as he held paper towels to his face. He recognized the boy as William Laufler, a ninth grade basketball player. "What happened to you?" asked Coach in bewilderment. "Do you need help?"

The boy shook his head. "I just got in a fight with Matt Donaldson. I'm okay, though."

"Where'd this happen? What started it?"

The boy groaned again. "It was outside, off school property." He tossed his head back to keep his nose from bleeding. "Let's just say I said the wrong thing to him. It was my fault."

Matt Donaldson was a very quiet boy. Like Stevie Reynolds, he'd been wrestling since he was five-years-old in the county youth league and had also won a junior national championship. Although only an eighth grader, he was as much a champion as Stevie or Eddie Gilbert. Most people would say that Matt was an extraordinary athlete, a brilliant honor roll student, and polite almost to a fault. But the rules of his parents were clearly defined, and there was little margin for error. So the next morning when he told Coach he couldn't go on the trip, Coach sort of laughed and studied his brown eyes for some hint of a joke. But Matt's face showed no sign of humor. He was much too serious about life to play any jokes.

"I went home last night and my mother saw blood on my clothes and knew I'd been in a fight," confessed Matt.

"I know. I talked to William after the fight," Coach told him. "But he said you were off school property."

"I know, but I lied to my mother," Matt admitted. "I told her I had a bloody nose from practice but she knew better. I'm not grounded for fighting, but for lying."

"Maybe I could call your mother tonight, Matt," suggested Coach. "You're a key player."

"She won't change her mind."

"What in the hell started the fight?" asked Coach, his voice lowered.

"William said something bad about my girlfriend, so I popped him," shrugged Matt. What was he supposed to do?

"Good that you popped him, bad that you lied to your mother," was all Coach could say.

24

Coach Waters stood in the middle of the locker room, whining and moaning to Jimmie Ray as we collected our wrestling gear for the first overnight trip. "What a way to open our dream season," he said over and over. "Three starters out! We might not even finish with a winning record in Beckley! Why did this have to happen? Why?" he kept asking.

Everyone else smiled. "Coach wouldn't be happy if he didn't have something to worry about," laughed Evan Whalen.

"Don't worry, Coach, I'll pull you through!" mimicked Doug Sillex in a heavy voice. "I'm going to go crazy! I'm going to go psycho on everyone!" he said, beating his chest. "Me *Psycho*! Me afraid of no one! *Psycho* win for Coach Waters!"

Everyone was laughing and hooting except Coach. His face showed no humor in keeping three starters back home. Jimmie Ray had a more realistic approach to the problem. "This will be a good test to see how good we really are. We win six, seven matches, we'll be happy. A little adversity never hurt anyone," he said philosophically.

"Oh, cut the crap, Jimmie Ray!" whined Coach. "It's not supposed to be like this!" and we all cracked up again.

* * * * *

If Jimmie Ray thought the Beckley tournament, with our team minus three starters, would be a good test to find out how good we really were, he was certainly correct. Even good teams seldom go through an entire season without adversity, but the truly great ones will often use the adversity as a springboard to even greater success. This was the opportunity to prove ourselves.

We took deep breaths and tried to relax as we prepared for our first match. "This is when we find out the truth. We can't afford three or even two losses if we're going to set the record," Tyler said to me in a serious tone as I sat down next to him.

I laughed. "You worry too much. It's not that important. I mean, it *is* important, but it can't be done. It's asking too much."

Tyler stared straight ahead and saw nothing. *You're damn right, it is important. And it can be done,* he thought to himself. This was a once in a lifetime opportunity to do something that people would remember him by. He wished Danny was here. He missed his best friend, who at least understood his desire to be a part of something great. Tyler sat contemplating the dream that had suddenly become very important to him. He had feelings like anyone else. It was selfish, he knew, but he wanted to be remembered for something. He was being realistic. Time wasn't on his side.

Tyler got up and walked over to Ryan Astrayka. "Sometimes things get dumped in your lap, and it's up to you to come through," he counseled the seventh grader who would be wrestling in Chris Galford's starting spot. "Just believe in yourself and you'll do fine."

"Did something like that ever happen to you?" Ryan asked.

Tyler thought back. "I started as a seventh grader because we really didn't have anyone else to wrestle. I stunk. But in the last match of the season, against Mecklenburg when the team really needed me, I stepped up," he said proudly, remembering when Coach Waters had bumped him up a weight class. Coach had *believed* in him. And Tyler had come through for him. In the back of his mind, Tyler knew that he would one day come through for Coach again. He didn't know how or when, but he knew it would happen.

The tournament would also be an opportunity for Tommy Johnson to redeem himself in Danny Schneider's starting slot. Last year he had finished only 7-12 as a part-time starter. But if Ryan and Tommy failed—and they were both basically unproven—we would be in huge trouble. And regardless of how they did, there was no one to fill in for Matt Donaldson. This meant we would have to forfeit his weight class in every single match. The only one worrying more than Coach Waters about our depleted lineup was Tyler.

The gym had four mats spread across the floor. There was a constant stream of people going backward and forward alongside the mats. It was an exciting atmosphere. The place was packed. Like so many southern West Virginia gyms, it had originally been a super high school built by the coal companies that ruled our state for so many years. When the coal companies began downsizing, the population loss had resulted in many high schools having to consolidate. Some had become junior highs. But when your school was often the only fabric that tied your community together, you clung to what you had left and you supported it. It didn't matter if it was a high school or a junior high school. For some people, it often meant driving a hundred miles down a narrow, winding road to support their team. After all, this was West Virginia, and sports and community spirit went hand in hand.

As things turned out, Tyler had spent much too much time worrying about our patched-up lineup. We cruised through our five matches on Friday, with the closest one being a 58-24 spanking of Shady Spring. The only real surprise was that Artie Badger lost a heartbreaking 7-6 decision to East Greenbrier's monster heavyweight. It ended his streak of thirty-some straight wins going back to last season. But our team was 5-0.

The coaches had a parent staying in every hotel room that night and there wasn't any horsing around. There was a sense of responsibility, a seriousness, from the eighth and ninth graders that hadn't been seen in years past. Maybe some of us were actually beginning to buy into what Tyler had been saying for months. We could be a very, very good team.

* * * * *

"There's no telling how good we could be this year! Three starters out and we never missed a beat!" said Tyler excitedly, sprawled across one of the hotel room's two queen size beds. "I just know we're going to win our first big championship tomorrow!" Across from him, sitting up reading a magazine, was Travis. I sat on the edge of the bed watching television.

Tyler's father put down the newspaper he was reading in a chair. "You knucklehead! We've only wrestled five matches.

We've never beaten Sherrard, and that's who we start out with tomorrow. Beat them and then do your talking." He shook his head and went back to his paper.

Tyler turned to look at his father hidden behind the paper. "Yeah, well, I remember some old man once telling me that if you believe in yourself, good things will eventually happen to you."

Big Bill rolled his eyes.

25

I f any of Tyler's grandiose dreams of winning championships or having a state record team were going to come
true, they would certainly have to go through Sherrard
Junior High. We were scheduled to wrestle them in four different tournaments, and the sad fact was that we had never
beaten them before. But over the last ten years hardly anyone
else had beaten them either, with the Wheeling team compiling
an impressive 231-26 record. The only thing different about
them this year was that their affable head coach, Ralph Barnett,
had resigned to take a similar position at a small college up
north. The team remained in good hands with his long-time
assistant coach. They were still the cream of the best, and you
could say they owned West Virginia junior high wrestling.

On the second day of the Beckley tournament, however, it
was Harpers Ferry who owned Sherrard. If Coach Waters was
waiting for us to choke or fall apart the way we so often did
the year before, he need not have worried. It never happened.
Our team was all business. Even when we had to forfeit six
points from Matt Donaldson's weight class, no one bothered to
look at the scoreboard. We blasted Sherrard, 56-24, and in the
process established ourselves as a team not to be taken lightly by
anyone.

Next in line was Braxton County. They had a new coach this
year, a *woman* coach. The boys on her team called her "Coach

Sal" and seemed to like her, but our guys kept looking at each other with the same question written on our faces. *A woman coach?* For wrestling, of all sports? Every now and then she would look over at our team as she studied her lineup in a corner of the mat. She appeared uncomfortable and out of place, but her seriousness gave her an intimidating look. The other coaches peered at her curiously.

Braxton won only two matches against us. One was a pin against Jake Patton, who was having a rough tournament and making it sound like everyone's fault but his own. The other was the forfeit in Matt Donaldson's weight class. But Braxton had an exciting match when their 95-pounder, a boy named Justin Digby, went against Tyler. He had blond hair and was well muscled, but angry-looking. The kid took Tyler down quickly and rode him hard in the opening round. "Hold him, Dig! Don't let him go! You can do it, Dig!" screamed the woman coach.

The boy, Dig, was still in control until he tried to reach his arm around Tyler's head. Tyler saw an opening and slipped his arm under Dig's armpit and snapped his shoulders around, driving them to the mat. Just like that, it was over. Pin.

"Shit!" yelled the boy, holding back tears as the referee raised Tyler's arm in victory. He was wheezing from the beating Dig had given him, but a win was a win. Dig started to head back to his bench but the woman coach pointed him over in the direction of Coach Waters. He walked over to Coach with his head down, slapped at his hand, then turned away without saying anything as he threw his headgear to the floor and stormed out of the gym. The woman coach's eyes followed him out the door, but she didn't get up.

We continued to beat down the Braxton County boys, but except for Dig, each of the losing boys would come over and shake Coach Waters' hand after the match. It wasn't until the 145-pound match that Dig came back into the gym. The woman coach immediately motioned him over and whispered in his ear as she pointed to Coach Waters. The boy put his head down and walked around the edge of the mat to Coach Waters. "I'm sorry for what I did, coach," he apologized. "I was wrong."

"That's okay," smiled Coach Waters. "What's your name, son?"

"Justin Digby, sir," he answered, looking down at his feet.

"You've got the makings of a fine wrestler, Justin," Coach told him. "Don't get down on yourself. You'll walk the halls of your school one day as a champion."

The boy looked up at Coach and smiled for the first time. He went back to his team and said something to the woman coach. After the match the Braxton boys were gracious in defeat, even smiling and offering words of praise as they lined up to shake our hands. When their coach shook hands with Coach Waters, she pulled him off to the side.

"First, I want to apologize for our boy being rude to you and throwing his head gear," she began. "I'm the behavior teacher at Braxton. I've been working with Dig to find something he can be good at, where he can feel good about himself," she explained. "Secondly, I want to thank you for what you said to him. You made his day." She paused and looked over to where

Tyler was talking with Dig and trying to demonstrate a move. Dig was smiling. "Everything about your team is top-notch, coach."

We continued to mow everyone down, running past Cameron Junior High, 62-21, and Point Pleasant, 59-31. We still hadn't had a close match and were 8-0 going into our final match against host Beckley-Stratton. But Beckley wouldn't be a pushover. They were 7-1 with their only loss coming in a closely contested match against Sherrard. And everyone knew that if Beckley won, they would be awarded the championship based on head-to-head competition. How many times in the past had we been in this position and failed?

* * * * *

We got off to a bad start against the Beckley boys, dropping three of the first four matches, but it was Tyler who helped bring our team back. He already had a cold and his lungs had been getting more and more congested since the morning. In his last match against Point Pleasant, he had to go the full distance before topping his opponent. There wasn't much left in his tank, but he kept telling himself he could make it through one more match. With our team trailing 15-6, he never thought of not wrestling. Big Bill started to say something to Tyler, but when he saw the determined look on his son's face, he knew no words of encouragement would be necessary.

Tyler was all over the Beckley boy from the beginning. He kept putting the boy's shoulders to the mat but couldn't score the pin, and by the end of the second period his breathing was heavy. His father motioned for an injury timeout. When Tyler ran off the mat, Big Bill held a cup to his son's face and slapped him hard on the back. It nearly knocked Tyler off his feet. A huge chunk of dirty brown mucus popped out of his lungs into the cup. Tyler took a deep breath and looked up at his laughing father. "Could you have hit me any harder?" he asked sarcastically.

Big Bill bent down and whispered in Tyler's ear. "You handled that like a wussy, but I guess I'll keep you anyhow, you little knucklehead."

Tyler smiled at his beaming father and raced back to the mat with renewed vengeance. He was wrestling on pure determination, but didn't have the strength to finish the boy off. The match ended with Tyler winning 12-4, good for four team points but not the six a pin would have brought.

The match between our schools seesawed back and forth. But every time we would inch closer to Beckley, the southern team would pull away again. The score remained close until Mike Thomas was unexpectedly pinned at 128, followed by the forfeit of Matt Donaldson's 135-pound class. Suddenly the score was 42-19 with only four matches remaining. Once again it looked like we were going to self-implode when a championship trophy was within our grasp.

Coach Waters had done the figuring. Quickly he called over Evan Whalen, Doug Sillex, Smitty Smith and Artie Badger.

"Here's the long and short of it, guys. We've got to pin our last four matches to win. Anything less, even a tech fall, and we lose the match." He looked discerningly at the four boys. "Nothing less than a pin," he repeated.

Evan smiled confidently. "Don't worry, Coach. I already scoped my guy out. I'll pin him, guaranteed." It took Evan less than a minute to be good to his word.

Coach turned to Doug. "Keep it going, Doug. This is our chance. You can do it!"

"Relax, Waters! Me Psycho, remember?" he said coolly. "Psycho afraid of nothing! Psycho get pin for Waters!" He promptly went out and pinned his opponent, forever earning the nickname Psycho.

Coach looked at Smitty as he put on his headgear for the next match. If Smitty had any doubts going through his head, he didn't show it. He looked at Coach with a slight grin. "I'll win it!" he promised, then turned it into reality with a first period pin.

Now all the pressure was on Beckley-Stratton. Artie may have lost to the East Greenbrier boy, but no one expected him to lose again. Not a single boy was sitting down. Every boy from both teams was standing, as well as just about everyone in the stands. The drama was unreal. We all knew that Harpers Ferry's day had finally come.

Quiet, dependable Artie did what he's always done. He methodically manhandled his much heavier opponent, pushing him around on the mat, holding him so tightly it looked like the kid was going to pass out. It didn't take long. Artie soon had him on his back and eyed the ref with clear hazel eyes. When the referee brought down his hand, the gym exploded. Beckley-Stratton had fallen, 43-42.

We had just won our first wrestling championship.

26

Our wrestling team was the talk of the school the next week as students kept stopping by the office to admire the championship trophy. It was the first trophy any of the teachers could remember. For the wrestlers, it was like being on a natural high. And with Matt Donaldson, Danny Schneider and the *Little Beast,* Chris Galford, all returning to the lineup, optimism abounded.

"I don't want to see any swelled heads!" thundered Coach Waters each day in practice. "You're only as good as your next match! We've got a big tournament this weekend with a lot of damn good teams! Fall on your faces and we'll be the laughing stock of the state!"

Tyler Moore spoke up in a serious tone. "No one's going to be laughing at us this weekend, Coach."

"We don't let no one laugh at us!" shouted the *Little Beast* in support.

* * * * *

Tyler's father had been called out of town on emergency business, so Tyler asked Jimmie Ray if he and Danny and Travis could ride up to Wheeling with him and Coach Waters. "Sure," grinned Jimmie Ray. "You can fill Coach's ears with all the state records we're going to set this year. It might help him relax a little."

Tyler narrowed his eyes. "You've got to believe," he replied.

When our caravan of cars and trucks got to Sherrard Junior High, Coach made everyone wait in the parking lot. "Now listen carefully," he said when everyone was assembled. "We're going to walk in, single file, one after another, as one long blue line," he told everyone, referring to the navy blue warm-ups that had *"Harpers Ferry Wrestling"* on the front and *"No Excuses"* on the back. That was the theme for our team, *"No Excuses."* Don't talk, just go out and do it.

"Why does Coach Waters want us to go in like this?" asked a seventh grader.

"I think I know," nodded Tyler with a big smile. "He wants everyone to take notice of our team. He wants to send a message to everyone, and maybe us, too, that we've got a very special team. If we all pull together, we could have a season that will go down in history."

Danny and I were standing behind Tyler as he spoke with glowing words to the little seventh grader. "You're crazy, Tyler," said Danny. He rolled his eyes.

I rolled my eyes, too. "You and your dreams."

"You've been waiting a long time to do this, haven't you?" Jimmie Ray asked Coach Waters as our team began lining up in formation.

"Ever since our first tournament here, when the Sherrard team walked in single file," agreed Coach. "It was an awesome sight, totally intimidating. Yeah, I've been waiting a long time to do this. This could be a very big year for us."

"You've been listening too much to Tyler."

Past the bleachers overflowing with local fans from Sherrard and Moundsville, the coaches led us through the gym, one by one. You could sense the hush that fell over the gym. On and on our line went, seemingly never-ending from the entrance of the gym to the locker rooms in the far corner. Everyone stared at our team. It was impossible not to be impressed.

"You happy now?" grinned Jimmie Ray.

"Best parade I've ever seen," Coach said proudly.

Maybe Sherrard was trying to get back at us for beating them the week before. Our first match was against Moundsville, their county rival and a perennial state power. Last year they were the only team to beat Sherrard, costing them a 40-0 season. And like Sherrard and Mecklenburg, they had that certain mystique about them that can be very intimidating to other teams. Moundsville knew we were riding high with a perfect 9-0 record, and though the season was still very young, the match would give the winner an early claim to state dominance.

Coach decided to keep Ryan Astrayka in the lineup, moving him up to the 80-pound class to replace David Carter, who had been ineffective. Tommy Johnson, after a terrific performance in Beckley, was also back in the lineup at 110, but so was Danny Schneider at 116. He was taking over for Ricky Stillson after he screwed up in the locker room. Coach had been going over some pre-match instructions when it happened.

"You guys in the lower weight classes, wrestle defensively. Don't get pinned," Coach Waters began. "If we can hang with Moundsville until we get to the bigger weight classes, we can take them." His eyes scanned the locker room and fell on Ricky.

"And you, Ricky," he continued, pointing a finger at him, "cut out the fancy moves you learned from the youth league. Just wrestle the way we taught you. Stick to the basics."

"What the hell's wrong with using my moves from the youth league?" he wanted to know. "They work."

"You're not Stevie Reynolds," Coach told him bluntly. "Sometimes your moves work and sometimes they don't. And when they don't work, you end up getting your butt pinned. We can't afford that today."

"I'll do what I want," he said sullenly.

Coach put his hands on his hips and stared at Ricky. Very calmly, he said, "No, you won't, Ricky, because you're not wrestling today with that attitude." He looked over at Danny Schneider. "Think you can handle wrestling at 116?"

Danny nodded quietly, his eyes avoiding Ricky.

"He ain't taking my place in the lineup! I'm wrestling at 116!" shouted Ricky. He stood up to face Coach Waters.

"Sit down, Ricky!" ordered Tyler, standing up. "You heard, Coach! You're not starting! Get it through your head! If you don't want to be a team player and listen to the coaches, we don't need you!"

Everyone's mouth dropped open. We'd never heard Tyler talk like that before. Geez, he wanted our team to win so badly. But he got the message across. Ricky put his head down and moved to an opposite corner of the room to sulk in private.

"Remember, you little guys wrestle defensively. Let our big guys do the hammering!" Coach shouted, pumping us up. "We wrestle as a team today!"

Danny Schneider, in particular, took Coach Waters' words to heart. Giving up a lot of weight, Danny was wrestling a great match until he screamed out during the third period. He clutched his wrist as Jimmie Ray signaled a timeout. It was plain to see he was in pain as the coaches examined his hand. "I can finish the match!" insisted Danny, who was only trailing 3-1. "I'm not going to forfeit!"

A local paramedic joined Jimmie Ray and Coach Waters at the edge of the mat. "It doesn't look good," he said, turning Danny's wrist over. "It may even be broken."

"It ain't broken and I ain't coming out!"

The paramedic looked at the coaches and shrugged. "If he thinks he can keep going..."

Danny didn't win the match, losing 5-1, but he wasn't pinned. And while Moundsville won seven of the first ten matches, none were by pins. All three of our wins were by pins. Moundsville's golden opportunity to get us on the ropes had passed by, and with them leading only 21-18, our *"Big Guns"* made their move.

Matt Donaldson, back in his parents' good graces, scored a tight 7-3 win in his first match of the season. It was all downhill from there for Moundsville. Evan Whalen took a major 12-4 decision, while Psycho, Matt, and Artie all scored pins. The devastating 43-21 loss left Moundsville reeling and fueled our momentum for the rest of the tournament. Even injuries couldn't stop us.

Psycho Sillex would be lifted off his feet and slammed to the mat in the next match against Edison. Though he won the match, his bell had clearly been rung. Poor Psycho walked around in a daze trying to remember who he was and where he was.

"How's Psycho feeling?" asked Coach Waters.

Doug grunted. "Uuugg, me not care about Psycho person. Me not feel well." He sat out the next two matches, replaced by Dennis Wilson, who stepped up and scored a pair of pins.

And Danny Schneider, refusing to come out of the lineup, would go on to wrestle two more matches that day, pinning both his opponents. By then his wrist had swollen so badly that the paramedic insisted on taking him to the hospital. X-rays revealed a fractured wrist. But our team had finished the day with a 4-0 mark, and like old times, we were tied for first place with Sherrard.

27

The next morning our team easily rolled over Independence, just a shadow of the team that had given us fits the year before. We then took aim on Summersville Junior High and polished them off, 74-6. Next up was Braxton County, the school with the woman coach. While we were warming up, some of the Braxton boys came over and asked questions, and before long we were all rolling around on the mats together. Coach Sal came over and stood next to Coach Waters. "I've watched your team and like the way they mix with the boys on other teams. I encouraged my boys to try and pick up a few pointers from your kids," she said. "I hope you don't mind."

"Course not," smiled Coach. "It's good to see they can be friends first and opponents second. I wish it was that way with our county rivals."

"I've heard about the Mecklenburg team," she said, her eyes dropping. "It's a shame there's so much bad blood."

Though the Braxton County boys showed some marked improvement from the week before, they were no match for us and fell, 51-21. Tyler once again beat Justin Digby, but he didn't pin him. And when Dig went over to shake Coach Waters' hand after the match, he wasn't cussing.

We were now one victory away from our second championship in a week, but having to wrestle Sherrard in front of their home crowd was a daunting task. You would never have known that Sherrard had their butts kicked just a week earlier by the way they were mowing everyone down. Their new coach must have planned it this way, because the rematch with Sherrard was the very last match of the tournament. The whole place was watching. Both teams were 7-0 and last week meant nothing.

The *Little Beast,* Chris Galford, proved his mettle once again by quickly pinning his opponent. Sherrard never got close after that. We never let up. By the time we got to the meat of our lineup, the *"Big Guns,"* we already had the match won. The match ended with Matt Donaldson, Evan, Psycho, Smitty and Artie all winning by pins. The Sherrard wrestlers fell like dominoes. With the hometown Sherrard fans now silenced, everyone else cheered on the most stunning, and worst, loss in Sherrard wrestling history. The final score was an absolute 75-9 thrashing of what had been the greatest junior high wrestling power in West Virginia history. Sherrard's record now stood at 15-2 with both losses to Harpers Ferry. At 17-0, Harpers Ferry stood on top of the mountain. Our team was real.

For the moment, the world belonged to Harpers Ferry. But the ride home would take some of the boys through an entirely different world.

* * * * *

It had been snowing lightly during the tournament, but certainly nothing to worry about. Everyone was excited as Tyler, Danny and Travis all piled into Jimmie Ray's car with Coach Waters for the ride home.

"So, Coach," asked Travis, "do you think Tyler will see his dream come true?"

"You mean about winning forty matches this season?" asked Coach Waters with a chuckle.

"It's all he ever talks about. He wants so much to be a part of something big, something that will always be remembered," laughed Travis, giving Tyler a friendly jab in the ribs.

For the next two hours everyone laughed and told jokes as the snow fell harmlessly around them. Things changed an hour past Morgantown. Interstate 68 can be a beautiful drive, especially through the Cumberland Valley. But when you're driving up high mountain peaks and looking down at the valleys far below, the sight is enough to make you dizzy. There are guardrails along the sides of the highway, of course, but you always have the feeling that if you go through them you will fall forever into a bottomless pit of empty space.

During the winter, the weather in the Cumberland Valley can be very unpredictable, and deadly. As the car roared up the mountain, the snow suddenly began to pick up, and within minutes the little scattering of flakes had turned into a raging blizzard. Danny and Travis had fallen asleep in the back seat, but Tyler could sense that Coach Waters and Jimmie Ray were getting increasingly worried the further they drove.

"What the hell's wrong with your windshield wiper, Jimmie Ray?" asked Coach as the snow and ice began to pile up on the window.

"My defroster ain't working right," he said. "I've been meaning to get the damn thing fixed."

"Well, ain't this a helluva time to think of it!"

"That ain't the worst of it," admitted Jimmie Ray with a shudder. "I've got a bad right front tire that has a bubble in it. The tire's off balance and could go at any time."

"For crying out loud!" exclaimed Coach Waters. "Why didn't you get it changed?"

"Because I don't have a spare."

"You're putting me on!"

"No."

Tyler peeked up over the back seat and looked out the front window. He couldn't see anything. It was a whiteout. The road was gone. No lanes, no markings, just snow and more snow. It didn't matter that snow and ice were crusting up on the windshield. You couldn't see beyond the hood anyhow. Coach Waters turned around and looked in the back seat. His face was white.

"Jimmie Ray, we got the boys," he said quietly. "We ain't gonna make it."

Long silences followed between the two men. When they did speak, their voices were filled with uncertainty. "Stop at the next hotel if you see one," Coach said. "We can't go on like this,

Jimmie Ray. We'll never make it. If your tire blows or we go off the road, we're done." Coach took a deep breath. "This is a nightmare!"

Tyler closed his eyes and thought of his home on Blue Ridge Mountain with his mother and father. He wished like he had never wished before that his father could somehow materialize to protect him and take him home.

Coach Waters kept muttering about the windshield wipers and tire bubble. His eyes were focused on the blinding storm as he tried to navigate for Jimmie Ray. Tyler didn't smile when Coach added a few choice comments about Jimmie Ray's mentality as they inched forward through the storm. He knew they were in trouble. The car crested the top of the mountain.

"My God! My God in heaven!" yelled Jimmie Ray excitedly. "I don't believe it! It's a miracle!"

From the back seat Tyler cocked an eye open to see Coach Waters give Jimmie Ray a slap on the shoulder. He was almost crying. "Pull in at the next gas station, Jimmie Ray! Pull in and stop!"

Tyler pretended to rouse himself from sleep and looked outside. There wasn't a snowflake to be seen. Not in the sky. Not on the road. The sky was moonlit and clear with stars everywhere. Jimmie Ray pulled off the interstate into a gas station. He and Coach Waters got out of the car and looked up into the sky as if God himself was looking down on them.

"There isn't one snowflake on the ground!" Jimmie Ray said in amazement. "I ain't gonna believe this for the rest of my life!"

Coach Waters began laughing a stupid, delirious kind of laugh a person makes who's just had the shit scared out of him and is suddenly safe. "It's like we passed through the Twilight Zone, from one world to another!" he exclaimed.

"God was looking after us! He was taking care of us!" Jimmie Ray exalted, still in awe. "Maybe it's His way of telling us we're going to have a magical season!"

"Hey, what's all the commotion?" asked Danny, stirring next to Tyler.

"God just blessed our season," Tyler told him, raising his eyebrow at Jimmie Ray.

28

The next tournament was just before New Year's Eve, six hours away in Charleston, the state capital. It was being hosted by McKinley Junior High, a team that had beaten us the year before. But our team ran into problems before we even left.

"Where's Ryan Astrayka?" Coach Waters asked, checking off boys as we began to arrive for the trip. "Anyone know where he is?"

"Uh, he had to go out of town to visit his grandmother yesterday," answered Ronnie Dillow shyly.

"Why didn't he let me know?" demanded Coach.

"Uh, I think he was afraid you'd get mad," came the reply.

"No kidding! And where's Ricky Stillson?"

Another player cleared his throat. "He had to go see his brother graduate from boot camp tomorrow."

"Boot Camp!" roared Coach. "Boot Camp! What about the team?" Coach knew he was in trouble. Danny Schneider was already out of the lineup with a fractured wrist.

"Not to be the bearer of more bad news," Artie Badger's father broke into the conversation. "We're still driving down to Charleston, of course, but I'm afraid Artie can't wrestle."

"Art, I don't need any funny jokes right now," Coach said irritably.

"No joke," his father said. "Artie took a slam at the Sherrard tournament last week. The doctor told him yesterday not to wrestle again until after the New Year. My wife would kill me if I let him wrestle." If it was up to Artie, he'd wrestle with two broken arms.

Coach Waters turned to Jimmie Ray. "I knew things were too good to last," he said. "Why are we even bothering to show up down there?"

Jimmie Ray pointed to a water fountain. "Take your pill, Mac."

Then it started snowing. Mr. Crawford, the principal, was at the gym to send the team off. As soon as he saw the snow he made Coach call Charleston for a weather report. They were calling for light snow. Jimmie Ray didn't want to take his old car until he had it fixed, which he still hadn't done, and had made plans to ride with Bill Moore and Tyler. Coach was going to ride with Stevie Reynold's mother and a few other wrestlers. The threat of snow changed all that.

Mrs. Reynolds said she couldn't drive if snow was in the forecast but still wanted to go. Coach Waters just wanted to get on the road before Mr. Crawford said they couldn't go. So when Artie's father offered to cram everyone into his huge travel van, Coach quickly accepted. It was a decision he would long regret.

Mr. Badger is a big, swarthy man with white hair and a very devout Mormon. No smoking, no drinking, no gambling or anything else that's fun. Little Artie was Big Art's pride and joy. He was either an accident or Big Art was simply determined to keep pumping away until he had a son, because when Artie was born he already had five sisters.

Riding to Charleston in *"Artie's Ark"* as the players had long ago dubbed it, was fun for everyone except Coach Waters. It was a nightmare for him. He wasn't riding with his old partner Jimmie Ray, and Art was certainly no Jimmie Ray to ride with. Vicki Reynolds was used to driving with Art to away matches. He always kept a few oral tape recordings of a classic book in the van and together they would listen to it on their drive. After every couple of chapters they would turn the book off and discuss what had transpired since their last discussion.

"Theoretically, I believe that Veronica was really in love with Frederick and was hoping that she would somehow break off her engagement with Ambrose," said Vicki.

"I beg to disagree," replied Big Art. "I think we'll find that Veronica's love for Ambrose will become stronger, perhaps by an unforeseen circumstance."

"No, I think her true love is Frederick, and that time will prove that. Turn the book back on so we can find out what happens next."

On and on it went, but the boys never heard a word. We were in the back of the van listening to music and roughhousing around with the team's young volunteer coach, Roland Proctor. Coach Waters, on the other hand, sat up front behind Art and Vicki and had no choice but to listen to the entire book. He was miserable.

Art kept warning us about roughhousing in the van, but no one paid him any attention. We were jumping from side to side in the van, landing on top of each other, that sort of stuff. You could feel the van swerve from the shift in weight. The snow was really coming down hard when we were still three hours outside of Charleston. The roughhousing continued. Finally Art stopped the van in the middle of the highway and turned around. His days of being a good Mormon were over. "I'm going to come back and kick the shit out of the next boy who moves another inch, and then I'm going to drag his ass out of the van and run over him! Is that clear?"

Travis turned around and looked out the back window. Cars were whizzing past both sides of the van. "This is not a good place to be stopped," he whispered to Chris Galford.

"I'm going to be a pancake in a minute," mumbled the *Little Beast*. He took a deep breath and gave a smile of thanks when Mr. Badger started up the van.

The rest of the trip was quiet, but dangerous, as the snow kept falling. Coach leaned his head against a window, shaking it every now and then, wondering how Art put up with this every week. The air in the back of the van began drifting to the front in heaps of gaseous fumes. We had gotten tired of listening to music and turned our attention to a farting contest. Coach covered his mouth and gagged. He never rode in Artie's Ark again.

29

The next morning our team drove over to McKinley Junior High, which was actually in a small town just outside the city limits named St. Albans. It's a rather saintly name for a town that is lined with one porno store after another. Everywhere you looked were billboards advertising strip clubs, slot machines, gay bars, and *"the best porno stores in the state."* Anyone who was still asleep from the night before was wide-awake by the time we got to the school

"Man, what a great place to live!" more than one boy was heard to say.

"Wow, this is like having everything in your own back yard," said Pyscho Sillex.

"I'm gonna move here when I get older," agreed another. It was pretty unanimous.

Coach Dave Walker of Independence was talking with the McKinley coach when our team entered the building. "Well, I'll be damn! I didn't expect to drive all the way here just to get my ass whipped again!"

The McKinley coach smiled at Coach Walker and replied, "We're not as strong as last year."

The Independence coach gave him a puzzled look. "I'm not talking about your team. I'm talking about Harpers Ferry. They're kicking butt everywhere they go. We're not going to beat them and neither are you!"

It was originally planned to be a six-team tournament, but both Point Pleasant and Sherrard backed out because of the snow. It was a curious thing about Sherrard. Only two days after we delivered a major butt whipping in front of their hometown fans, Coach Waters received an e-mail from the new Sherrard coach. He said they had to back out of our season-ending tournament at Harpers Ferry because of *"limitations on out-of-area trips."* It was kind of funny because Sherrard had built its reputation as a state power by being able to go wherever they wanted, whenever they wanted.

Even with Ryan, Danny, Ricky and Artie out of our lineup, our team never missed a beat. Coach Waters worked his magic by juggling our wrestlers around in the lower weight classes. He also moved up Smitty Smith to Artie's spot, while Dennis Wilson took over for Smitty at 165.

We steamrolled Hays Junior High 60-23 and Dave Walker's Independence team, 64-19, before gaining revenge on McKinley for last year's loss at Braxton County, 54-27. It was another total team effort with the *Little Beast,* Tyler, Stevie, Matt Donaldson, Psycho and, shockingly, both Dennis Wilson at 165 and Smitty Smith at heavyweight, all going undefeated.

Hey, we were 20-0. Anything was possible.

* * * * *

Tyler and his father had planned on stopping in Petersburg to visit Tyler's grandparents on their way back to Harpers Ferry. Jimmie Ray and Coach Waters both caught a ride home with

Smitty Smith's mother. Coach Waters would have taken a bus back rather than ride in Artie's Ark again.

After leaving his grandparents' house in Petersburg, Tyler and his father drove up and down the mountain roads as Tyler tried to pull in radio stations that faded in and out. "Hey," cried Tyler excitedly as a station came in crystal clear. "That's my favorite song!" It was the John Denver hit that brought West Virginians together, "*Country Roads.*" Tyler listened to the words, his head bobbing to the song's rhythm.

"*Almost Heaven, West Virginia. Blue Ridge Mountain, Shenandoah River...*"

"I remember the first time I heard that song. I was about six-years-old and you took me to Morgantown to watch a West Virginia University football game."

Mr. Moore groaned at the memory.

"After West Virginia won the game, the loudspeaker began playing *Country Roads* and everyone stood up and sang along with it," Tyler continued happily. "It was just so neat when all the people did that and I've loved the song ever since. It's like the national anthem of West Virginia," he giggled.

"I know," his father said. "And you tried to sing the damn song all the way back home. The problem was that you only remembered two or three lines, and you kept singing them over and over again. You about drove me crazy."

"You know, Dad, every time I hear that song, I can't help but think it was made just for us. It's all about the Blue Ridge Mountain and Shenandoah River. And everything is so beautiful that it really is almost heaven."

"My son, the nature lover," moaned Big Bill.

Tyler listened to the final words of the song. *"Take me home, down country roads,"* he repeated, turning to his father. "That's us right now, Dad. You're taking me home, down country roads." He laughed.

"You *are* a genuine knucklehead," his father said, giving Tyler a worried look.

Tyler laughed again.

As they drove down country roads towards home, they talked about Tyler's dreams. "Do you think we'll get forty matches in this season?" he asked. "It'd be nice to win them all."

Mr. Moore smiled. "First you want to win forty matches, now you want to go undefeated. Don't you think you're asking for the stars?"

"If we can just get forty matches in, we can set the record."

"That's not going to be easy. One team didn't make it to the Sherrard tournament last week and two more got snowed out at McKinley," his father reminded him. "Another snowstorm and we won't get the matches in. And if we do get forty-one or forty- two matches in, there's not much room for error."

"I really don't think anyone can beat us. Not our team. If we can get all the matches in, the record will be ours." He leaned back in the seat and closed his eyes. He wanted this so bad.

"Suppose you go undefeated at 39-0?"

"It wouldn't be the same," Tyler said. "Two high school baseball teams won 39 games a long time ago, and then Sherrard won 39 matches last year. I researched it."

Big Bill reached over and turned down the volume on the radio. "Winning forty matches would be sweet, but they say all records are made to be broken."

"Not this one," Tyler insisted. "High school teams are now limited to a maximum of thirty-nine games in a season, counting playoffs. And with all the junior highs being turned into middle schools, there won't be any more junior highs. A record set this year will stand forever."

"So why is it so important? You've got lots of time in your life to make accomplishments."

Tyler looked at his father without smiling. "No, I don't, Dad. You know it and I know it. I can pray for a miracle that they find a cure for cystic fibrosis, but it may be too late for me." He drew in a deep breath. "I used to think that no matter how often I got sick, I'd always get well. Now I know better. I'm not afraid of anything, but there's something inside of me that keeps telling me I don't have a lot of time to waste."

"Tyler..."

"Don't you want your life to stand for something?" Tyler asked. "Even if it's something little, like being part of a state record team?"

"But, Tyler, you're life does stand for something. You're my son and I'm so darn proud of you. Remember how you didn't win until the last match of the season as a seventh grader? Hell, I thought you might never win a match." He covered his eyes and shook his head at the thought, a big grin on his face. "Now look at you two years later. How many matches have you won this year, fifteen?"

"Sixteen," corrected Tyler quickly.

"The point is, I'm so darn proud of you just the way you are, son. I wouldn't trade you for any kid in the world, not even one that behaves."

Tyler didn't laugh. "It's not the same," Tyler said to his father. "Twenty years from now, I want other kids to look at our team picture. I want them to point to me and say Tyler Moore was on the greatest state record team in history. And I want Grandma and Grandpa to be able to say their grandson helped do something that will never be done again." He looked out the windshield at the snow swirling around in the headlights. "I know it sounds selfish, but I want to be *remembered* for something!"

30

We were beginning to get some pretty decent write-ups in the local newspaper. Surprisingly, while Mecklenburg had a team again this year, there had been very little news about them in the month of December. Apparently the whole state knew what had happened at our tournament last year because no one in West Virginia wanted to schedule them.

We continued our quest for the state record when we drove four hours to Buckhannon in the central part of the state the first weekend in January. By now it seemed that every parent wanted to drive, to be a part of the rolling bandwagon. There were high mountains to cross, so Jimmie Ray had borrowed his wife's SUV and all the coaches were going to ride together.

Tyler was going to ride in Artie's Ark with a zillion other wrestlers. Just before the team pulled out of the parking lot, he discovered he had left his uniform at home. This meant a twenty-minute detour up Blue Ridge Mountain for his father to retrieve it. You could say Big Bill wasn't none too happy about it. "You dumb little knucklehead!" he said with a shake of his head. "I'm surprised you don't want me to wear your jockstrap, so you don't forget it, too."

Tyler grinned. "Be happy you have me around. Not every kid is as lucky as me!" He knew some kids with cystic fibrosis didn't make it to fifteen.

Mr. Moore tousled his son's hair. The boy was his life. "You're still a dumb knucklehead!"

We blew past Grant County, 76-3, to open the tournament. Blennerhassett Junior High fell next, 76-6, with only Jake Patton losing. The poor guy couldn't wrestle. After a third straight blowout against Jackson Junior High, 78-6, we battled Buckhannon-Upshur for the pool championship. Buckhannon took three of the first four matches before we stormed back to sweep the rest of the bouts for a 66-12 stunner that left the host team dizzy.

We then took on East Fairmont for the tournament championship in a battle of undefeated teams. The East Fairmont gang was 19-0 on the season and, like our team, was brimming with the confidence that comes with being undefeated. They were strong in the lower weight classes and jumped out to a quick 14-3 lead. But it was Tyler who stole the show at 95 and kept our team from free-falling away. He was wrestling some kid who was undefeated, a little tank with huge muscles and a compact build. The boy had been wrestling forever and had a big reputation. Maybe it was Danny Schneider, back in the lineup with his wrist healed, who pulled Tyler through.

The East Fairmont kid tossed Tyler around like a doll, quickly getting him on his back. Danny kept screaming at him not to give up, though a couple of times it looked like the ref's hand was going to come down for a pin. Danny was standing behind the team bench yelling so loud his voice carried halfway across the gym. "Don't give up, you little wussy! You're wrestling like a baby! Don't give up, you wussy!" On and on it went.

It was clear Tyler had heard Danny. When he finally worked his way back to get on his knees, the first thing he did was flip Danny the finger. Fortunately the referee didn't see it, although there is some question whether a wrestler can be penalized for flipping off his own teammate. With thirty seconds remaining, Tyler pulled a reversal and put the Fairmont boy on his back for a one-point lead. Danny continued to scream *encouragement* to Tyler as he held onto the kid for dear life, trying not to let him slip away.

"Hold him, Tyler! Hold him, you wussy!" yelled Danny. "Don't let him go!"

Our team watched Tyler in amazement. He was giving this kid everything he had. He was barely hanging on and finally screamed out, "He's too strong! He's too strong! I can't hold him anymore!" I'll never forget that. It was like a cry for help, but there was no one to help Tyler except himself. But hold him Tyler did, and when the match ended, Tyler had a one-point win. If the match had gone on another two seconds, I doubt he would have won. That's how tired he was. But he was used to pushing himself beyond his limits. He was a boy who simply didn't know how to quit at anything. When he got back to the bench, Danny wrapped his arm around him and gave him a hug. His eyes were filled with pride for Tyler. "You little sunavabithch! You little sunavabitch!" he repeated. "I love you, Tyler!"

Danny and Tyler. Best friends for life.

Tyler's win stunned East Fairmont. He had beaten the team's best wrestler, and their guys looked at our team with dazed faces. Maybe it just sucked the wind out of them. Or maybe it would have been impossible for any Harpers Ferry boy not to have given his best effort after that. Oddly enough, the only boy who lost after Tyler's match was Danny. The final score was 57-17. It was our closest match of the day.

With four tournament championships already behind us, we had turned into a wrestling machine of ungodly proportions.

31

Coach Waters waited until Sunday night to call in the wrestling results from Buckhannon. He correctly assumed the Sunday paper would be full of basketball scores that he wasn't interested in reading about. It proved to be a good move. There was little in the way of sports news on Monday morning except for the screaming headlines:

Harpers Ferry Matmen Win B-U Duals,
Team Wins 25ᵗʰ Straight!

The story told about the individual wrestlers and our many accomplishments, including Stevie Reynolds who was 25-0. With a 92-3 lifetime record at Harpers Ferry, he was closing in on the state junior high career record of ninety-seven wins, held by none other than Lenny Langston's brother. Coach Waters and Stevie were both well aware of the record and the fact that Langston's brother held it. The day couldn't come fast enough for Stevie to break it. But we weren't a one-man team, not by a long shot. There were nine other boys on the team with at least twenty wins, including Tyler with a 20-5 slate. Matt Donaldson was still undefeated with a 16-0 record since missing the first tournament, and everyone else had at least fifteen wins except Jake Patton, who was lucky if he won at all.

The enthusiasm around school on Monday was unreal. It was like our team had won the World Series or Super Bowl, or both. Even the basketball players treated us with newfound respect, calling us "unstoppable" as they slapped us on our butts. It was turning into a championship season and everyone was feeling it. The school had never been united like this before, at least not since the old high school days.

"Hi, Tyler," came a soft voice behind Tyler in the hallway.

Tyler turned to see a seventh grade girl smiling bashfully at him. She was the same girl who had stopped him in the hallway last November and asked him if the wrestling team was going to set a state record. "Hi, Marsha," he said. He had quickly found out her name that day when she told him he was a good wrestler, but mutual shyness and different class schedules had limited their conversations.

"I heard you had a really terrific match on Saturday when you wrestled the boy from East Fairmont. The whole school is buzzing about it." She gave him a warm smile, and Tyler felt the blood rushing to his cheeks.

"Thanks." He didn't know what else to say. She had given him a golden opportunity to brag about himself, but he was suddenly tongue-tied. Wrestling was easier.

Marsha coughed. "I, uh, was wondering if you were going to the Sadie Hawkins dance two weeks from Saturday? It's the night after your last tournament."

Tyler was sure his cheeks were burning red. "I don't know," he said, trying to regain his composure. "I heard a girl was supposed to ask you out."

Now Marsha blushed. "Yes, Tyler. I was asking if you'd like to go with me." She hesitated. "I wanted to ask you out before someone else did."

Tyler had been to school dances before, but never on a date. "Sure, sure, Marsha. That would be great."

"Good," she said and headed up the staircase.

Both their cheeks were on fire from blushing.

* * * * *

The next day our team had a wrestling match against Mecklenburg in front of our student body. Unfortunately, the Future Farmers of America field trip to Morgantown was on that day. Since Jimmie Ray was the vocational teacher, he had no choice but to go. Bill Moore had signed up as a chaperone long ago, but they both assured Coach Waters that he and Roland Proctor would have no trouble handling Mecklenburg. Still, Coach was very unhappy about the whole thing. He had called Boss Parker over at Mecklenburg and explained the situation, but Parker had smugly refused to reschedule the match. But Coach Waters did make sure that Tyler and every other wrestler in the F.F.A. would be staying for the match.

Coach was frantic the morning of the match. Without Jimmie Ray or Bill to help him, he had to weigh in all the boys himself to be sure they would make weight in the afternoon. He was furious when Tyler and Danny didn't make weight. Tyler was nearly two pounds over. Coach told Danny to start running laps around the gym but told Tyler to get dressed. He stared at Coach. "Whaddaya mean, get dressed? I can't wrestle if I'm overweight!"

"No, you can't, Tyler. You'll have to sit this one out," he said wearily. "Two pounds is too much for you to lose. You'll run yourself into the ground trying. I can't take a chance like that with your, uh, illness."

"Like hell you can't! It's my life and I'm going to wrestle!" He began putting on his heavy warm-up suit.

"Tyler, your mother made it clear she doesn't want you cutting any weight. She's worried about your health."

"Yeah, and she's always treating me like a baby instead of letting me live my own life! That's why my parents are always arguing!" he fired back. "I want to be like everyone else! I can't live my life like I'm going to die the next day! This isn't your choice or my mother's choice, it's *my* choice!"

"Dammit, Tyler!"

Tyler finished lacing his shoes and moved past Coach Waters to join Danny in the gym. "Don't you have a class to teach right now? You're supposed to be there!" he said over his shoulder.

"God bless almighty," muttered Coach as he went upstairs to his classroom.

32

After lunch that day, Coach Waters led everyone down to the locker room to weigh in for the match. He hoped the new Mecklenburg coach would help put an end to the lingering animosity between the two schools. He tried to greet him warmly.

Suddenly the locker room door swung open and in strode Lenny Langston. "Hey, Waters," he said casually.

Coach turned around and did a double take. "What are you doing here?" he said in a disbelieving tone.

"I'm a volunteer coach," Langston replied with a smile.

"Does Boss Parker know about this?" glared Coach.

Langston laughed. "Yeah, Waters. He even gave me a ride here in his car. I have to take some recertification tests, but once I pass them, I'll be a paid coach again."

"You can't be a coach!" he insisted. "Boss Parker promised me that you and Butcher would never coach again!"

"Is that why Boss Parker personally drove me over here?" he smirked smugly. "I think he's trying to tell you something, Waters."

Coach was rattled and it showed when the match began. When he looked across the gym floor, he saw Lenny Langston smiling at him with that big, smirky grin. Boss Parker was right behind him, arms folded and smiling serenely. Coach bit down on his lip and shook his head. He kept muttering, "They gave me their word. *They gave me their word!*"

Our team started out well, with the *Little Beast* and Ronnie winning by pins and Ryan Astrayka taking a forfeit. After Joel Patton got pinned, as usual, Tyler was up next and should have belted the kid. But he was so exhausted from running he could barely move and lost by points. At the 102-pound weight Mecklenburg had a hotshot kid named Marcus Devon who they touted as "unbeatable." The kid was real, taking Stevie Reynolds to the limit before Stevie put him away, 5-3. No more being unbeatable.

The gym was rocking now, especially with Tommy Johnson following with a quick pin. Danny had made weight and should have had an easy time with his opponent, but like Tyler, he was already exhausted from running. He put up a good fight and led his opponent 8-4 going into the last period, but he ran out of gas and got pinned. With five matches left and Mecklenburg forfeiting the heavyweight match to Artie, all we had to do was win one more match and it was over.

Matt Donaldson went out at 135 against a boy whose father had blasted Coach in the newspaper last year. Like most of the Mecklenburg parents, he didn't like us. After Coach Waters was quoted as saying that Butcher and Langston had cheated at our tournament, he wrote an open letter to the paper calling Coach *"irresponsible, vengeance-seeking, and a terrible role model by being such a poor loser that he would stoop to false accusations of cheating."* But Coach couldn't do anything about that. Roscoe Belcher had his hands tied, saying he'd better not write a rebuttal unless it was approved by the board office. And the board office wasn't going to do that. All the board office wanted was the "black eye" that Coach had given the school system to go away. The boy fought a lot cleaner than his father and put up a good fight, but Matt took him by a 7-4 score, clinching the win for Harpers Ferry.

Mecklenburg knew they were already beaten, but they still had their dirty work to do. Evan Whalen was up next and had to wrestle a kid who looked really defiant, like he had a major chip on his shoulder. The boy's name was Stratford. It wasn't pretty. Stratford cut Evan's mouth in the first period and Coach struggled to stop the bleeding. During the injury timeout, Lenny Langston took Stratford aside and kept making pointed jabs at his mouth, slowly twisting his hand so that his knuckles would roll across the boy's mouth. As soon as Evan returned to the mat Stratford went for his mouth, jabbing at it with a closed hand, his knuckles twisting across Evan's mouth.

Coach knew right away what was happening and yelled to the referee. The ref brushed off his protests. Blood started coming from Evan's mouth and again the match was stopped. But as soon as Evan returned to the mat, Stratford went straight for his mouth. He wasn't even trying to wrestle. He kept jabbing at Evan's mouth, almost like he was hitting him. "C'mon, ref, you gonna allow that street crap? The kid's going for my boy's mouth! That's dirty wrestling, and you know it!"

After the match was stopped for the fourth time with Evan comfortably leading 8-3, Evan ran out of blood time. You're only allowed two minutes of accumulated injury time during a match, and Evan's time had run out. He was forced to forfeit the match even though he had outwrestled Stratford up and down. With the smug jeering coming from the Mecklenburg bench, you'd have thought they had just beaten our whole team.

"Sorry, coach," said the referee. "Nothing I could do when your boy ran out of time."

Coach shook his head in disgust. "That was the dirtiest match I've ever seen in my life! You let it happen!"

"I didn't hear that," warned the referee. "I don't want to flag you!"

The next wrestler for Mecklenburg was pretty decent, but no match for Psycho Sillex under normal circumstances. But Psycho had been sick with the flu the last two days. Coach knew that he was drained and should have just forfeited the bout with the match already won, but Psycho was insistent on wrestling. He went out and got pinned in the final period after puking on the mat.

Mecklenburg took the next match, too, pinning Smitty Smith when he got nauseated thinking about rolling around on the mat where Psycho had just lost his lunch. It was a pretty ugly finish, in a lot of ways.

Mecklenburg had scored eighteen straight points, but on any other day we would have won all three matches easily. Artie took the last match by forfeit to make the final score 45-39, but everyone knew we should have stomped Mecklenburg by forty or fifty points.

* * * * *

After everyone got dressed, Coach led us upstairs to his classroom. The parents followed us. Coach had been seething ever since Lenny Langston had walked into our locker room with that big smirky smile on his face, and he didn't mince words with us for our poor performance. "You guys looked like crap today!" he began. "Maybe you read too much in the paper about how good you are! Maybe you thought all you had to do was show up, and Mecklenburg would melt with fright! We should have destroyed that team!"

Everyone looked down at the floor. Even the parents were surprised at the tongue-lashing the team was getting, especially after beating hated Mecklenburg. Then the real truth came out. "Mr. Waters," said Vicki Reynolds, listening quietly with the other parents. "I thought Lenny Langston wasn't allowed to coach anymore. Why did Boss Parker drive him to the match?"

"That's a good question, Vicki!" he angrily replied. "He was shoving it in our face! Telling us it's okay for Lenny Langston to openly cheat last year, and it's still okay to coach! Anything to win!" There was no stopping Coach. He drew in a deep breath. "I'll say this to everyone in this room," he said, raising his finger in the air. "I don't care if we had beaten Mecklenburg by fifty points today, we will *NEVER* wrestle them again! What happened to Evan Whalen typifies the way they coach! They lie, they cheat, they go back on their word, and they are the dirtiest team I've ever seen! I've had it! At some point ethical and moral standards have to come into play, and Mecklenburg has none! We are *FINISHED* wrestling them!"

"What about our next match with them?" asked Evan, checking the bloodstained cloth that he dabbled at his mouth. "I want that Stratford kid!"

"Forget it! I'm reminding Mr. Crawford they gave their word that Butcher and Langston were done coaching. That was the only reason we wrestled them. They lied to us! Hell, they'll probably have Butcher back for the next match, too! As far as I'm concerned, they broke their word and everything is off!"

33

The thought of not wrestling Mecklenburg again made Tyler anxious that night. He had checked the remaining schedule. If everything went perfectly, without wrestling Mecklenburg, our team would have fifteen matches left to go with the twenty-six matches we had already won. All it would take to end his dream of the state record would be having just two teams unable to wrestle. Why couldn't we wrestle Mecklenburg again? We'd crush them the next time, and we damn sure might need the extra match.

Tyler got on the internet and had more bad news. A couple of Mecklenburg wrestlers had posted how they had nearly beaten us, supposedly the best team in the state. If a few bad calls hadn't gone against them, they surely would have won. But they'd show the rest of the state how good they were when they wrestled Harpers Ferry in a rematch next week. *"We will get even, our time will come,"* read one ominous posting. Tyler knew that wasn't going to happen. Coach Waters had been very adamant about not wrestling Mecklenburg again, and the parents were completely behind him. It was like taking a sure win out of our hip pocket. But as Coach had said, the match had now become the focus of an ethical and moral issue. Enough was enough.

When Tyler was finished reading the postings, he went downstairs to talk with his father. He had earlier told him what happened at the match, from the time Lenny Langston walked into the locker room to Coach's tirade in the classroom. His father had nodded in agreement and said Coach wanted to make a point. It made sense before Tyler had gone over the schedule and realized there was no room to spare. Getting in every possible match was vital. Now he wanted to wrestle Mecklenburg again. Some chances were too important to pass up.

"Get your homework done?" Mr. Moore asked when Tyler walked into the cramped living room. He was reading the news-paper while his wife watched television in their bedroom.

"Yeah, not much to do," Tyler said without interest. He hadn't cracked a book and had two tests on Thursday. "Don't you think we should go ahead and wrestle Mecklenburg next week? After all, we did agree to wrestle them home and away," he asked hopefully.

Big Bill folded his paper and laid it on the coffee table. He looked at Tyler with raised eyebrows. "What's this all about?"

"We're supposed to wrestle them next week in front of their school," he began. "I'm sure all the students at Mecklenburg..."

"This is about the record, isn't it?" interrupted his father. "You don't give a lick about the Mecklenburg students. You just want the record, right?"

"What's wrong with that?"

"Nothing," admitted his father, "under normal circum-stances. But they chose to cross the line. Coach Waters had one simple request, that the coaches who cheated last year be banned from coaching. And Mecklenburg agreed. *They gave their word.*"

"But maybe Mecklenburg is just giving them a second chance."

Mr. Moore put his elbows on the table and leaned closer to Tyler. "Do you *really* believe that? Those coaches didn't cheat other adults. They cheated *kids!* What kind of role models are they? And after we agreed to wrestle them, you would have thought they'd have the decency to reschedule the match when Coach told their athletic director about our school field trip."

Tyler shrugged. "I don't think it's that big a deal. We'd beat them again, anyhow."

"One day, Tyler, you'll understand that the most important thing a person can have is his good word. If your word means nothing to you or other people, then you really have nothing of importance. What they did today was totally unethical. If I had been the head coach, I wouldn't have even wrestled Mecklenburg after Lenny Langston walked into the locker room."

"You feel *that* strongly about this?" Tyler was shocked.

"You're darn right I do," his father said evenly. "This is about integrity and principles, and doing the right thing. I think Coach Waters is trying to stand up for all the little schools that have been walked over by larger schools, like Mecklenburg, who think they have a license to do whatever they want."

"We can get back at Mecklenburg by beating them again," Tyler insisted, missing the point. "We all want that record."

"I don't think the record is going to come down to one match," grinned Mr. Moore. "Besides, you guys might lose the next ten matches in a row."

Tyler laughed back. "Fat chance."

"Remember, son," his father said, going back to his newspaper. "Sometimes you have to hurt inside before the important things in life really mean something to you."

34

O ur team left at noon on Friday for the trip to Roane County, over on the western side of the state. It was the fifth and last road trip of the season, and we were all growing weary. The coaches were together in Jimmie Ray's borrowed SUV, leading the way, with pickups and cars following close behind. Artie's Ark again pulled up the rear. It was like a traveling caravan.

Winter darkness can come early in the remote mountains of West Virginia. If you're traveling through unknown areas it can be depressing, or at least a time for deep thinking. Tyler sat next to Travis in Artie's Ark, and Travis had been unusually quiet. He stared out the window at the bleakness of the passing terrain. "Why have you been so quiet?" Tyler finally asked. "You've hardly said a word the whole trip."

"Everything looks so sad," Travis said without interest as he looked toward an imposing mountain in the distance. "Once you get off the interstate, everything is a winding, two-lane road that bends into nowhere." He shuffled in his seat. "Look at all the little houses and trailers we've passed. They seem to be standing all alone, with no one nearby. And high up on that mountain," he steered with his hand. "You see a couple of lights spread across the top. It makes you wonder how far those people have to go to the nearest store, or at least to find human companionship. What a lonely life it must be." He shook his head. "I don't know how people can live like that." Travis shivered in the warmth of Artie's Ark as the other boys bragged and roughhoused with each other.

"What else is bothering you?" Tyler knew something was wrong.

"I guess I'm just depressed, thinking about my father. He lives alone on a mountain. I was wondering if he was lonely, if he misses me and my brother and sister." Travis took a deep breath. "And you know what? He's never seen me wrestle."

Tyler winced. "That's got to be rough. I live for my father to see me wrestle. Heck, I missed him not seeing me against Mecklenburg, even though I lost."

"I just wish he'd get to see me wrestle once. I'll probably never wrestle again when I get to high school." Travis closed his eyes, and Tyler thought it was so he wouldn't be able see his tears.

* * * * *

The next morning in the town of Spencer, Jimmie Ray got directions to the school and everyone piled into the traveling caravan. Only a few townspeople were out in the chilly morning air, but those that were turned to stare at the stream of cars and trucks rushing past. The people smiled curiously and waved as if welcoming us to their town.

Everyone made weight again except for Tyler. It was ironic that Tyler was the only boy who had trouble making weight, because he was the only boy who couldn't afford to lose it. With his cystic fibrosis every pound was important, and it was the subject of endless battles between his parents. Naturally his mother was worried about her son and wanted to protect him. Big Bill wanted him to be like any other kid. Tyler just wanted to be himself.

Mr. Moore no doubt had reservations about Tyler cutting weight, but he knew Tyler was going to do it with or without his father's permission. Bill understood this. He couldn't just say, "Sorry, son, you can't wrestle," because that would hurt Tyler more than losing a pound or two. Besides, it was a good excuse for them to pig out together at McDonald's when a tournament was over. Bill always said that every moment he had with Tyler was precious, but that he wasn't going to baby him. The sooner he made his own decisions, the sooner he was going to live his own life.

Coach Waters watched as Tyler circled the gym with a determined look on his face. "He's tough," muttered Coach with admiration. "The boy will be something one day, given the chance."

Danny, Travis and I jogged along with Tyler to keep him company, and together we went back to the locker room for him to weigh in again. Tyler stripped off all his clothes and got on the scales.

"You knucklehead!" said Bill. "You're still an eighth of a pound over!"

"Uh, why don't you try this?" suggested the referee, knowing a few tricks. "Stand on your head for two minutes, then come back and try again." Tyler dutifully went to a corner of the locker room and stood on his head, wang hanging down, while everyone else turned away with laughter.

"That has to be one for the ages," Travis said.

"What Tyler won't do to wrestle," I marveled.

"I've seen it all now," agreed Danny, laughing so hard he had tears in his eyes.

After two minutes Tyler returned to the scales. "Turn your head and cough," the ref said.

Big Bill rolled his eyes. As soon as Tyler turned his head and coughed, the referee reached over to the weight ring and slid it back to zero. "Yep, that cough did it, young fellow. You just made weight," he grinned.

The ref certified Tyler and left the room while Tyler got dressed. "Gee, Dad, I didn't think I was going to make weight."

"Neither did I, you knucklehead!"

35

There were ten teams in the tournament, divided into two pools of five teams. Each team would get four dual matches. We continued to blast away our opponents with amazing success, sweeping past Edison Junior High 72-9, Clay County 77-12, DuPont Junior High 90-0 and Spencer 71-6. Our team was on a mammoth roll with no end in sight. The winners and runners-up from each of the pools then wrestled for individual places one through four. Counting both the varsity and junior varsity squads, we placed eleven wrestlers in the championship match and another six boys in the consolations for 3rd and 4th place. For any other school it would have been an amazing feat. The way we had been wrestling, getting more and more dominating each week, our accomplishment was almost expected.

There was one thing that happened, however, that wasn't expected. Stevie Reynolds had come into the tournament with a 93-3 junior high record, just four wins short of the state record held by Lenny Langston's brother. And though Little Red wasn't one to put personal goals above his team, he did want to have an undefeated season. As a seventh grader he had lost twice, then suffered a single heart-breaking loss last season when he finished 38-1. Now he wanted to run the table and go undefeated, something he had not done even when he won the peewee national championship.

Stevie easily won his first four matches in pool play to tie the state record. He still had to wrestle a boy from Wirt County in the championship round. One more win would not only give him another tournament championship, but the all-time West Virginia record. He had wrestled the boy from Wirt County, Nolan Dye, last year and beat him, but it had been a dogfight won by points and not a pin.

Things went smoothly until early in the second period with Stevie winning a tough battle, 3-2. Dye threw a cross-face to Stevie, a nice legal move, but his backhand brought blood from Stevie's nose. The referee called an injury timeout and Coach Waters and Roland were left to patch him up. Jimmie Ray and Bill Moore were at the other end of the gym coaching our wrestlers who were in the consolation matches, and with injury timeouts every second counts.

Coach Waters raced over to Stevie and reached into the fishing tackle box that served as a first aid kit. "Where are the tampons?" he demanded.

"For what?" asked Roland.

"They're perfect for stopping nosebleeds," Coach said as he rummaged through the box. He came up empty. "Hell, they must be in the other kit."

"We don't need a tampon, Mac," Roland said. "Gauze will work just as well." He began shoving it up Stevie's nose.

It became clear that the gauze was a distraction for Stevie. Not only did he have his hands full with Nolan Dye, but the gauze kept slipping out of his nose. Twice more Stevie had to use an injury timeout. The second time Roland frantically tried to tape his nose shut. By now Coach had sent Ronnie Dillow running to the other side of the gym for a tampon. When he got back, Stevie was on the mat with only a few seconds of timeout remaining. There wasn't time to use the tampon.

Stevie was in for the fight of his life. Dye was good, damn good, and you couldn't wrestle him and worry about bloody gauze coming out of your nose at the same time. Dye pulled a reverse on Stevie with twenty-five seconds left to take a 4-3 lead, then gamely held on as Stevie frantically tried to escape. The seconds ticked down, and with them went Stevie's undefeated season. Dye had won.

After they shook hands, Dye wrapped his arms around Stevie in a show of admiration for a match well fought, but Stevie put his head down and walked out the double doors. At the end of the tournament, Harpers Ferry had six champs, five runner-ups, and four third place finishers. Our varsity totaled thirty-eight team points to easily run away with our fifth team championship. Wirt County finished second with twenty-three points while our junior varsity squad finished a respectable fifth with seventeen points.

When it was time for the top three finishers in each weight class to get their trophies, Stevie was nowhere to be seen. His mother was still in the gym, visibly disappointed as she applauded when Nolan Dye's name was announced not only as champion of the 102-pound class, but also as the tournament's Most Outstanding Wrestler. Stevie's name was announced as runner-up, but Matt Donaldson had to go accept Stevie's trophy for him.

"I'm going to find Stevie," Jimmie Ray said harshly.

"Go easy on him. He's pretty upset," warned Coach.

"No."

Coach Waters nodded to the double doors where Tyler was heading. "I don't think you need to go," Coach said. "Let them play it out."

Tyler found Stevie sitting down in the gym lobby. His head was buried in his hands as he leaned against a brick wall. "I never thought I'd see you act this way, Stevie."

"It meant a lot to me to go undefeated. It's been my goal all year."

Tyler shook his head. "You know, we've had guys in the past, me included, who won only one or two matches *ALL* year, but they didn't act like you."

"Leave me alone."

"No. Did you know Matt Donaldson had to go accept your trophy for you because you're out here pouting, feeling sorry for yourself?" he said accusingly. "How about all those times you won a championship and your teammates were there to cheer you on when you got your trophy? Some of those guys have never won *any* trophies, but they were still cheering for you. Now when the tables are turned, you're out here sulking instead of being inside for your teammates." Tyler turned to go back inside the gym. "You didn't let yourself down, but you let your teammates down. And you're acting like a *stupid mountain brat!*" he added.

Stevie raised his eyes at Tyler but said nothing.

A few minutes later Little Red walked back into the gym. His face was still very red and his eyes watery. But he held his head high. He walked over to his teammates and began shaking hands with them, then went over to Nolan Dye who proudly showed him his Most Outstanding Wrestler award. Stevie looked at it and smiled, then gave Nolan a hug and patted him on the back.

*　*　*　*　*

Late that night, when the team arrived back in Harpers Ferry after another six hours of driving, Mr. Moore treated Tyler, Danny and Travis at McDonald's for burgers and shakes. "A lot of the parents were talking about our upcoming match with Mecklenburg on Thursday," Travis said between bites of his burger. "Do you think the match will be cancelled?"

"That's a tough call," replied Mr. Moore. "I know the coaches don't want to wrestle Mecklenburg because they lied to us. But I don't know if anyone has the backbone to stand up to Boss Parker."

"The parents say we should just not show up for the match," offered Danny.

"It's not that simple," Mr. Moore contended. "If we don't show up, Mecklenburg stands to lose a lot of money. They're counting on that money for their budget."

"I say just wrestle them," announced Tyler.

"One day you'll understand why the coaches are serious about not wrestling Mecklenburg, regardless of what happens to them."

"What does that mean?" Tyler asked with a worried look.

"It means I just don't know what's going to happen," Mr. Moore said with a deep sigh. He was exhausted from another long drive. "I'm afraid things could get very ugly."

36

The upcoming rematch with Mecklenburg had been hotly debated among the parents who were at the Spencer tournament. Everyone was incensed that it hadn't been immediately cancelled. "First, they cheated us last year, then they come begging to wrestle us again this year. We only ask that the cheating adults not be allowed to coach anymore!" Vicki Reynolds told anyone who would listen. "But they have to throw it in our face by having Boss Parker drive Lenny Langston to our match so he can coach against us. It's like they're above the rules and can do whatever they want. And what is the school board doing about it? Nothing! How are we supposed to teach our children right from wrong?" She had a very strong sense of what was right and wrong, and she made sure that all the parents knew how she felt. "The match needs to be cancelled!"

Boss Parker and Roscoe Belcher had other ideas. Despite an outpouring of phone calls to the board office from Harpers Ferry parents demanding the match be cancelled, Boss Parker held his ground. "You know, Huey, we would lose well over a thousand dollars by not having the match in front of our student body," he told his good friend at the board office on Monday afternoon. "Where is the fairness in canceling the match after we already wrestled in front of the students at Harpers Ferry?"

"If Mr. Waters had only minded his business last year, there wouldn't be a problem. It looks to me like Harpers Ferry is trying to stick it to you," he observed. "And they're trying to do it by saying it's all about their honor. But I truly think that your young coach deserves another chance."

Boss Parker laughed heartily. "Absolutely! Frankly, I'm getting tired of hearing all this bullshit about honor. But you might want to make a little trip to Harpers Ferry in the morning to be sure they understand that the match will go on as scheduled."

"You can count on that," agreed Roscoe Belcher.

* * * * *

It was 10:30 Tuesday morning when Coach and Jimmie Ray were summoned to the principal's office. It was like entering a mausoleum going into Mr. Crawford's brick office. No one spoke as he gestured for them to take a seat opposite Roscoe Belcher. The office was cramped with boxes of books lining the floor along the walls. Outside it was beginning to snow, adding to the silence of the room.

"Mr. Waters and Mr. Lawson, I want you both to understand in no uncertain terms that on Thursday your team will wrestle Mecklenburg. There will be no ifs, ands, or buts about it," Roscoe Belcher said without a greeting. "And you might want to tell your little army of parents to cease with their phone calls to the board office. They are wasting their time."

"This is about ethics and principles. When you give your word on something, you keep it. You go back on your word, you pay the price," Coach Waters told him without hesitation.

Roscoe Belcher only sneered. "Mr. Waters, those are very noble words. But I'd like to remind you that *you* will be the one paying the price if you don't wrestle Mecklenburg." He loved his authority.

By the time the meeting was over, the snow was coming down hard. At 12:45 Mr. Crawford made an announcement that school would be dismissing early in fifteen minutes. "Be sure to listen to the radio in the morning for any school delays or cancellations," he warned the students.

They were wise words, because there would be no school for the rest of the week, and certainly no wrestling match on Thursday. Our parents from Harpers Ferry saw it as fitting justice that the weather from God had intervened to keep the match from being wrestled.

Not only had the snow cancelled the wrestling match, but it also knocked out a full slate of boys' and girls' basketball games on both Wednesday and Friday. Semester exams were scheduled the following week, and no athletic contests or even practices were permitted until exams were completed. There had been no talk about making up the lost basketball games. With the end of the season only a few days away, there was no reason to believe the wrestling match with Mecklenburg would be rescheduled.

But Boss Parker had not become the powerful athletic director at Mecklenburg by allowing other people or other schools to have their way. Whether or not the match was held had suddenly become too big an issue in the county. There could be no compromise at this point. Because of Harpers

Ferry, the Mecklenburg wrestling team had been scorned throughout the state. And the little school certainly wasn't going to dictate what Mecklenburg could or couldn't do. He wasn't really concerned with the admission money for hosting the match, although that was his selling point to Roscoe Belcher and his friend at Harpers Ferry, Ben Duval. If for some reason the match wasn't held, he knew that Roscoe Belcher would see to it that the board office allocated the lost revenue to Mecklenburg at its next budget session. Boss Parker simply wanted everyone to clearly understand that he still ran junior high athletics in the county.

Our wrestling team had our first practice in over a week when exams ended the following Friday. It was also the day that Coach Waters had arranged for the team picture. At Tyler's urging, the photographer was going to blow up some photos to a mammoth 11"x14" size. Inserted across the bottom of each photo would be an inscription reading *"Harpers Ferry Wrestling, West Virginia State Record."* The only thing the photographer needed to wait on was our final season record. Tyler had it all figured out, and even told the photographer to reserve two blown-up photos, one for him and one for his grandparents.

There were still two matches against Virginia schools slated for Tuesday, followed by nine more matches at the season-ending tournament next Friday and Saturday. Our team would finish with forty-one matches if the weather didn't interfere, and Tyler was praying mightily that there would be no more snow until the season was over. He was sure that the good Lord would not allow anything to keep his dream from coming true. Certainly God had to know how important it was to him.

37

I t snowed again on Sunday, canceling school on Monday. If school was called off on Tuesday, the Virginia matches would automatically be cancelled and never made up. For once there wasn't a single boy on the team who didn't want to go to school the next day. There was a two-hour delay the next morning for the county school system, but there would be school. Both the Virginia schools were in session, and both schools were coming to Harpers Ferry for the afternoon matches.

Our team wrestled Clarke County at 4:30 that afternoon, and most of the students had stayed for the match even though school had been dismissed at 2:45. Parents, alumni and people in the community joined the students. A surprising number of shop owners in town had even closed early so they could attend the event. The fans who came were not disappointed. We crushed Clarke County, 68-9, then followed it up with an 84-0 drubbing of Timber Ridge, running our season record to 32-0.

Against Clarke County, Stevie Reynolds eclipsed the state record for most career wins held by Lenny Langston's brother. There wasn't much fanfare for Stevie. About the only thing he ever wanted out of wrestling was to have an undefeated season, but that wasn't going to happen. So when he became West Virginia's all-time junior high winner, he just shrugged.

With the final tournament only days away, the school was buzzing with everyone talking about setting the state record. The only thing that could stop us now was the weather. No one even considered the possibility we might lose. The thought of winning forty matches *and* going undefeated was almost beyond belief. Those last practices on Wednesday and Thursday before the tournament were especially bittersweet for the ninth graders. Many of us had been a part of the team since seventh grade and knew we would probably never wrestle again. "It's hard to believe that this is the last practice we'll ever have," Travis said as we went through our stretching exercises. "I just wish my father had seen me wrestle."

"For three years we've practiced and played together," Danny said, his voice trailing off. "And on Saturday, it's all going to end."

Tyler smiled at his friends. "That's why it's so important to set the record. People will talk about us long after we've stopped wrestling." He closed his eyes at the thought.

"Tyler and his dream," chided Travis.

There were fifteen minutes left during Thursday's final practice when Coach Waters and Jimmie Ray were called to Mr. Crawford's office. There was a questioning look on Big Bill Moore's face as the two coaches left the cafeteria, and even the players knew that something was wrong. The coaches returned just as the mats were being rolled up for the last time. They went over and talked quietly with Tyler's father for a few minutes as Mr. Moore shook his head.

"Everyone against the wall," Coach Waters shouted. He didn't look happy as he nodded to Jimmie Ray. "You tell them. This makes me sick." His cell phone rang and he went outside the cafeteria to answer it.

While everyone paid attention, Jimmie Ray pawed the floor with his foot. "We're going to wrestle Mecklenburg next Wednesday."

Psycho squinted his eyes. "What? You've got to be kidding! Our season is over Saturday!"

Jimmie Ray shook his head. "There's nothing we can do about it, short of resigning."

"You ain't going to quit, is you?" asked the *Little Beast* with a defiant tone. "That ain't right! No way!"

"That's bullshit!" said Evan Whalen hotly. "Someone needs to stand up to them!"

"We'll stand up to them!" shouted the *Little Beast.* "They can't cheat us no more!"

Tyler looked at his father. "Dad, you always taught me to stand up for myself, to do the right thing. What are the coaches going to do?"

Big Bill looked thoughtfully at his son. "If we refuse to wrestle Mecklenburg, none of us will coach again. That came from the school board office. But it's a decision we'll have to make."

"Mr. Crawford warned us that if we resign there's no coming back," added Jimmie Ray.

"Like Lenny Langston didn't come back?" asked Tyler.

Coach Waters walked back into the cafeteria holding his cell phone, a deep frown on his face. "I'm afraid we have more bad news. Coach Sal just called me. They're having a big snow storm up in Braxton County and have already called school off for tomorrow. They won't be allowed to come to our tournament."

"Swell," said Big Bill. "That knocks us down to ten teams and we can't wrestle our junior varsity squad. It leaves us with eight matches. If another team backs out of the tournament, we won't have a chance to win forty matches."

"Unless we wrestle Mecklenburg next Wednesday," implied Matt Donaldson.

"I want that record!" yelled the *Little Beast.*

"This is no longer about a record," said Coach Waters. "The whole point in not wrestling them is to stand up for our principles. We want to show them that you can't give your word on something and then go back on it. Your word must stand for something."

"And one day you guys will learn the importance of standing by your word," agreed Big Bill. "If we finish this tournament with thirty-nine wins because someone else gets snowed out, I'd still rather resign than be forced to wrestle Mecklenburg. So would all the coaches. That's how strongly we feel about this."

Tyler narrowed his eyes at his father's words. "You're really going to resign, aren't you?" he asked pointedly. He looked around at his teammates. "Would it be okay if we had a closed-door meeting in the locker room? Without the coaches?"

38

"We all know how the coaches feel about not wanting to wrestle Mecklenburg," Tyler said when everyone was in the locker room.

"You heard what they said. We don't have a choice," offered Stevie Reynolds as he unlaced his shoes. "They'll get fired it we don't wrestle."

"No," corrected Tyler. "They said *they* don't have a choice. We do."

"What are you getting at?" Artie Badger asked. "We can't just say we're not going to wrestle."

"Suppose another team gets snowed out tomorrow," said Evan Whalen with a frown. "We'll *have* to wrestle Mecklenburg to get in forty matches."

"I want that damn record!" screamed Chris Galford. The *Little Beast* was hell-bent on getting the record.

Danny pulled off his T-shirt and winced at the smell. He dropped the shirt on the floor and began spraying himself with deodorant. "Tyler, all season long you've talked about getting the record. It was our chance to stand for something and always be remembered. What gives?" He looked down at his T-shirt and kicked it further away.

Tyler stood up to address us. "For a long time that record *was* the most important thing in my life," admitted Tyler. "But now I'd rather be remembered for something more important, and that's standing by our coaches." His eyes swept over his teammates. "You think our coaches don't want the record? Of course they do!" he said emphatically. "I want the record, too. We all do. But it means nothing if we turn our backs on the coaches who got us here. These guys are willing to resign, and probably never coach again, because they're trying to teach us the importance of having values and standing by our principles."

Tyler went on to explain what he had in mind as we listened in silence. "You're crazy, Tyler, but you make sense," Psycho Sillex told him. "I'm with you."

"I don't think the coaches are going to like this," Evan Whalen said.

Tyler looked straight at him. "Tough! My dad says that sometimes you have to hurt inside before the important things in life really mean something to you."

Evan rolled his eyes. "Okay, I'm in," he nodded. "You have my word."

"You have my word, too!" shouted Chris Galford. "*The Beast* don't go back on his word like Mecklenburg!"

"But if one person decides to back out, the whole deal is off," Stevie Reynolds said somberly. "Some people may feel differently after the tournament. We can't let this split our team. It has to be unanimous."

"Unanimous," everyone agreed.

Friday morning was gray and overcast with a biting wind that tumbled the temperature below freezing. But it wasn't snowing, and members of our team breathed a collective sigh of relief. We ate together on the first lunch shift and were given a rousing send-off by the other students. We were all seated at long, reserved tables in the center of the cafeteria, each wrestler with an individual name card. The basketball players and cheerleaders led the other students in silly, but funny, good luck cheers. And the talk never stopped about how we were going to set a state record. It would be a record that would never be broken and put little Harpers Ferry on the map forever.

"Good luck at the tournament, Tyler," said Marsha, who was supposed to be in math class. "I'll be at the high school to root for you as soon as school is out. I know you'll do super."

Tyler gulped. "Thanks, Marsha. Everyone's pretty excited. This is the neatest thing that's ever happened to me."

"How many wins do you have so far this season?" she asked, her eyes bright.

"Twenty-five," answered Tyler like it was no big deal. "I should get my thirtieth win on Saturday." He hesitated. "Will you be there on Saturday?"

"I wouldn't miss it for anything," she promised. "You haven't forgotten about our date for the Sadie Hawkins dance tomorrow night, have you? It will be a great way for *us* to celebrate."

"Sure, sure, Marsha," he gulped again, his face turning red. "It'll be a great way for *us* to celebrate," he repeated after her.

"You're a real champion, Tyler," she cooed, and for the third time in less than a minute Tyler found himself gulping.

The high school gym looked huge when it was empty. As the other teams began arriving, everyone pitched in to tape down the mats, pull out the bleachers, and bring concessions from parents' cars, anything to help out. When everything was ready, we killed time by rolling around on the mats together as we waited for the last team to arrive. Some of the coaches from opposing teams, along with Jimmie Ray and Roland, were out on the mats demonstrating moves to boys from other teams. There was a sense of camaraderie among everyone. It was a loose, easy feeling that made Coach Waters and Bill Moore smile.

"Look at the way those boys get along," marveled Big Bill. "Some of them live hundreds of miles apart, and they act like they've known each other for years."

"Too bad the people in our county can't get along like everyone else," lamented Coach Waters. "It's like a constant war between the two sides of the county."

"It's like the Harpers Ferry people aren't good enough for the Mecklenburg people. It's been that way forever," said Bill with a sense of resignation. "We're just a bunch of mountain brats to them."

"And it will probably continue to go on like that," responded Coach with a nod. "At least until someone from Harpers Ferry puts a little mountain magic on the people of Mecklenburg."

Both men laughed, but it wasn't funny.

"Hey, Mr. Waters!" called out a student running up to him. "There's a phone call for you in the main office."

Coach Waters gave Bill Moore an annoyed look. "Always some parent calling about something. We'll get this tournament started as soon as the Mannington team arrives."

Ten minutes later Coach walked back into the gym with a drawn look on his face. He motioned for all the coaches to join him around the tournament director's table and gave them the bad news. "I was just on the phone with Coach Burdette of Mannington. Their bus slid off the road on Sideling Hill up in Cumberland. Some of the boys were injured and taken to the hospital. Nothing real serious, but there were some cuts and broken bones," he explained. "The coach said the county is sending out another bus to take the team back home. They won't be able to make the tournament."

Dave Walker of Independence looked relieved. "At least no one was seriously injured," and the other coaches nodded.

"Might as well get the tournament going," said the East Greenbrier coach. "Everyone else is ready to go."

Coach looked over at Jimmie Ray, Bill Moore and Roland Proctor. He knew what they were thinking. "We're not going to get forty matches in without wrestling Mecklenburg," remarked Roland.

The coaches looked at each other, their minds crisscrossed with emotions.

39

We easily cruised through our four matches on Friday to raise our season record to 36-0. But the same thought went through each wrestler's mind that day. There would be only three more matches the next day, with no chance of setting the state record. We constantly stole glances at our coaches throughout the afternoon and evening, trying to read their minds. No one had *really* thought it would come to this. But we had also made a pledge to each other, and it made us fidget nervously as we thought about it.

As the gym began to thin out at the conclusion of Friday's wrestling, Mrs. Reynolds stopped Coach Waters. "Steven told me that you might turn in your resignation if you're forced to wrestle Mecklenburg on Wednesday. The other parents are behind you a hundred percent. We think it's admirable that you're trying to teach the boys about respect and honor."

Coach nodded sadly. The record would have been nice, but there would be no turning back.

There were no surprises at the tournament on Saturday, except for Travis. He had just finished pinning his opponent in the first match against Blennerhassett Junior High when he heard, "Way to go, Travis! Keep it up!" Even before he turned to see his father in the stands, Travis could hear him proudly shouting to everyone around him, "That's my boy! That's my boy!"

Travis scrambled off the mat and went into the stands to give his father a big hug. He didn't care how old he was or how silly he looked, the man was his father and he had just seen him wrestle! Damn!

Travis's father looked just like Travis, only taller. "When the tournament is over, I want to take you and your mother and little brother and sister out to eat at any restaurant you want! This calls for a celebration!"

"Dad, I didn't think you were coming. I thought your work was too important to miss..." he said, his voice trailing off.

Mr. Nutter smiled at his son. "I *thought* my work was too important to miss until your friend Tyler called me. *Then* I realized that nothing was more important than seeing my son wrestle." He nodded down at Tyler on the mat. "Your mother pointed your friend out to me earlier. He's quite a person. He has a real knack for understanding what's really important to people."

Coach Waters went over and introduced himself to Mr. Nutter. As Travis came back to our team, he could hear Coach telling his father about all his accomplishments and what a fine young man he was. It made Travis feel giddy with happiness. His giddiness would turn to pure energy because he would go on to pin his next two opponents with his father watching. And by the time his last match was over, *everyone* would know who Travis was by the way his father kept hootin' and hollerin' for him. Hearing his father yell for him gave Travis goose bumps, the best goose bumps he ever had in his life.

After roughing up Blennerhassett in the first match, we cruised through our next match in a ho-hum manner, blowing past Warm Springs 71-14. We were 38-0, with one more match against East Greenbrier. It turned out to be almost boring, a going-through-the-motions type of match. Some of the younger boys on the team were running around and screwing off, not really paying attention. The excitement of having a perfect season was missing. Everything was so methodical. Take your man down, put him on his back, pin him. Boom, boom, boom. The coaches looked at each other, then at the ceiling, waiting for the sky to fall, but everything continued in an easy, carefree manner. It was Harpers Ferry's day in history.

In fitting fashion, Artie capped off the final match by pinning his opponent from East Greenbrier. It was the same boy who had beaten him in the first match of the season to hand him his only loss. When the referee's hand came down Harpers Ferry was 39-0, and the gym shook. Parents came streaming down from the stands, and we began jumping up and down, hugging each other and giving out high-fives. It was instant madness. Then we all ran to the center of the mat and sprawled our bodies down, extending our hands out into a circle as we let out one final yell of victory, *"39 and 0! 39 and 0! 39 and 0!"*

The only thing left unknown was the slated match against Mecklenburg on Wednesday, but everyone knew it would be decided before anyone left the gym.

As we crowded around our coaches to offer congratulations, Tyler stepped forward and bluntly asked, "What have you decided about Mecklenburg? Are you going to wrestle them or are you going to resign?"

His words rang out like a gunshot.

40

Coach Waters looked at Jimmie Ray, then Bill, then Roland. They all nodded. "Everyone knows how we feel about wrestling Mecklenburg, and why," he said, looking around at all the boys and parents who were listening in. "Everyone knows what happened last year. They begged us for a second chance, to show that things would be different. All we asked is that the two men who cheated the kids last year be forbidden to ever coach again in this county."

The parents began nodding their heads and murmuring their approval. Our team looked closely at Coach Waters. Some of us dangled our headgear loosely by our wrists. Others began shuffling their feet quietly as we waited for his next words.

"Mecklenburg gave us their word that these coaches would never coach again," continued Coach Waters. "By bringing back one of their coaches, they made a mockery of us. They wanted to show us they were above everything, including integrity."

"That athletic director hand-delivered Lenny Langston," spoke up one parent. "Drove him right to our school, he did."

"But wasn't that agreement made in front of Mr. Belcher and the principals and athletic directors of both schools?" asked another parent. "Why was it allowed to happen? Why are they demanding we wrestle Mecklenburg when the season is over?"

"It's all politics and the lack of a backbone by some people. We're not playing their game anymore," interrupted Bill Moore. "If we don't take a stand here, it will never stop."

"But we also know how important it is for the boys to finish the season undefeated with forty wins," added Jimmie Ray, grinning at Tyler. "It will be their chance to go down in history." Tyler sheepishly looked off to the side but smiled.

"So the coaches have decided to turn in our resignations to protest the match, and the way the school board has handled everything. But the match will go on," Coach said matter-of-factly. "We'll have Mr. Duval coach the team, but we won't be there. After the match is over, I'll write a letter to the newspaper outlining everything that happened last year and this year, and let the chips fall where they may."

"But you won't be allowed to coach again if you turn in your resignation, isn't that right?"

"And you could even lose your teaching job if you write a letter to the newspaper?"

Coach Waters looked at his wrestlers. "Sometimes you have to do what you have to do," he said, and the other coaches nodded in agreement.

Everyone listened in silence, and then our team walked away to the locker room.

It seemed we stayed in the locker room forever, but no one had left the gym. Finally, one by one, our team began emerging from the locker room as we headed toward the far entrance of the gym where the coaches stood next to Mrs. Reynolds and the other expectant parents. Tyler led the long procession with

Stevie Reynolds at his side. Stevie nodded to his mother, and she began looking for something in a bag she carried. It was reminiscent of the long march the team took earlier in the season at Sherrard, like a big parade, but this time we weren't wearing our uniforms. Instead, each boy carried his uniform in his hand. As Tyler and Stevie approached the coaches, Mrs. Reynolds pulled out a large black garbage bag and opened it next to the coaches.

"I'm quitting the team, Dad," announced Tyler, dropping his uniform in the bag. "We had a great season, didn't we?"

Mr. Moore eyed his son carefully and proudly. "You big knucklehead. You're still supposed to wrestle Mecklenburg on Wednesday."

Tyler shook his head and addressed the coaches. "There's no need for anyone to resign now. You don't have a team to wrestle. The school board can't make us wrestle when we've already quit."

"What about the record?" questioned his father. "Being the only team to win forty games or matches? That's all you've talked about for six months."

Tyler shrugged his shoulders indifferently. "A wise man once told me that sometimes you have to hurt inside before the important things in life really mean something to you."

Big Bill hugged his son. "You dumb knucklehead! I'm so proud of you!"

Stevie Reynolds stepped in front of Tyler and dropped his uniform in his mother's outstretched bag. "I'm finished, too," he said to the coaches. "We realized there are more than just records to life." He stepped aside to make room for the players behind him.

"Are you sure you guys want to do this?"

"It was unanimous," Danny Schneider informed him, dropping his uniform next.

The coaches stared silently at each other, then at each boy as we placed our uniforms in the opened bag. It was our way of showing the coaches we had learned the meaning of integrity even if it came with a price. All of us could see the deep lines of appreciation etched in our coaches' faces as they nodded at each passing boy. It was a sight that sent chills down the spines of the watching parents.

When we had finished filing past them, the coaches looked at the bag full of uniforms. "What they just did means more to me than any record in the world," remarked a stunned Bill Moore.

"It had to hurt them to give up the record," said Coach Waters.

"They just walked off the top of the mountain for us," said Jimmie Ray in astonishment.

41

The day after the tournament Tyler and Danny went hiking with Marsha and her friend, Carrie. They had all had a great time at the Sadie Hawkins dance and decided to spend the following afternoon hiking in the area. Up the steep mountainside across from Harpers Ferry where the Potomac and Shenandoah Rivers joined together was the perfect place for a long hike. A trail led to a rock outcropping at the top known as Maryland Heights. It offered a spectacular view of Harpers Ferry from the other side of the Potomac River and the neighboring mountains of Virginia across the Shenandoah River. It was not an easy hike.

Mr. Moore picked up the girls at Marsha's house and began peppering everyone with questions about the dance. "Did you get Tyler to dance last night, Marsha?" he asked as Tyler squirmed in the seat next to him.

Marsha's eyes sparkled as she looked at Tyler. "He's a good dancer, Mr. Moore," she replied, playfully squeezing his hand. "Although it took him a while to get the hang of it."

"Thank goodness it didn't take him as long as it did to win his first wrestling match," chuckled Tyler's father. "Or you'd still be at the dance trying to teach him."

Tyler sank low in the front seat. "Can we please just get to Harpers Ferry?" he wondered as he rolled his eyes. He was blushing again.

"I wasn't too good a dancer myself when I was your age," went on Mr. Moore. "But after a while I could really kick up..."

"Dad, pleeeeeeze."

A short time later Mr. Moore dropped them off in Harpers Ferry. "I'll be back at four to pick you up," he said as they got out of the truck. "Have a good time, kids."

"You have a really nice father," Marsha said appreciatively.

"He acts like we're little kids," Tyler said stubbornly as the four teenagers made their way across a railroad bridge to the Maryland side of the river. They stopped and put their hands over their eyes to peer up the mountain at the peak far above them.

"This leads to the top," indicated Danny, pointing to a single lane path that led into the brush. "There's a wider path about fifty yards upriver that's easier to walk and doesn't take as long."

"I've gone this way a lot of times," said Tyler, gesturing towards the path. "I like the challenge."

They had a difficult time making their way to the top, climbing over rocks and helping each other along narrow ledges. The wind blew colder the higher they went. After nearly an hour, Tyler's breathing had become forced. Danny suggested they turn back, but Tyler shook his head and kept repeating. "We're almost there. I'm not quitting now."

When they finally broke into the clearing at the top, the view was stunning. "Oh, Tyler!" gasped Marsha. "This is amazing!"

"Sometimes a little hard work makes it all worthwhile," huffed Tyler.

Danny and Carrie walked over to the far edge of the rock outcropping and sat down to enjoy the scenic view of the Virginia mountains on one side. Tyler and Marsha huddled together on the other side and looked down over the town of Harpers Ferry, which now seemed so tiny below them.

"I'm so glad we came up here," Marsha said, nuzzling against Tyler.

He pointed across the river. "See that big rock up on the hill behind the church?" he asked. "That's Jefferson Rock. Thomas Jefferson said from that spot the view is so beautiful that it was worth a trip across the Atlantic Ocean just to see."

"Do you come up here often?" she asked.

Tyler smiled thoughtfully. "This is where I come to do my thinking," he answered. "When I'm up here, it seems that anything is possible. It gives me hope that one day I can lead a normal life like anyone else."

"Do you know why I like it up here?" Marsha asked.

He shrugged. "Because you can see all of Harpers Ferry?"

She gave him a shy smile. "Because I'm here with you, silly," she said with contentment. "Tyler, you're a very special person."

"Even with my illness?"

"Maybe that's what makes you so special. You don't know how to give up at anything."

"I just want to be normal, like anyone else."

"You're too special a person to be like anyone else."

Tyler breathed in the cold air and looked up at the blue sky. "At times like this I wish I could live forever, but right now I feel like I'm already in heaven." He leaned over and gave Marsha a kiss. It was his first kiss.

*   *   *   *   *

Tyler had a difficult time sleeping that night. Even though they had taken the easier route back down from Maryland Heights, it had still been tiring for him. And when the girls wanted to visit all the old shops that dotted the historic district, he had willingly gone along with a smile on his face. But inside, his lungs were filling with mucus. By the time his father picked them up he was heavily congested. Although he tried to tell his parents at dinner about the wonderful time he had with Marsha, he had trouble swallowing his food and talking was difficult. His parents knew the warning signs, and a check of his temperature confirmed he was running a fever. They sent him to bed early, and Tyler did not try to argue.

It was nearly three o'clock in the morning when Danny Schneider awoke to blue lights flashing around the walls of his bedroom. Something was terribly wrong. He threw off his covers and hurried to his window to peer out. At the Moore house, up the road, an ambulance was sitting in the driveway. Danny didn't wait. He jumped into his clothes and grabbed his jacket, slamming the front door behind him. He raced to Tyler's house and began banging on the side of the ambulance. A door swung open and an arm reached out to pull Danny inside. Then it sped off into the Blue Ridge Mountain darkness.

42

Danny Schneider's mother drove him from the hospital to Harpers Ferry Junior High at 10:30 Monday morning. The announcement came over the school's public address system at quarter after eleven for members of the wrestling team to meet in the auditorium. All of us mumbled on the way to the meeting. We had already made our decision not to wrestle Mecklenburg and Mr. Crawford or the school board couldn't force us to wrestle. The meeting was a waste of time. But when we walked into the auditorium, we immediately knew that something was wrong, something far more serious than a wrestling match. Coach Waters stood at the front with his back to the door, a hand shielding his face. Jimmie Ray Lawson sat in a chair, a look of disbelief on his face. He motioned for us to sit down without speaking.

Coach Waters finally turned and stared helplessly at our team. "It is with terrible sadness that I have to tell you..." he paused, his voice cracking. "That Tyler Moore died early this morning of serious pneumonia-like symptoms. His lungs were flooded with mucus. He just couldn't breathe anymore."

Everyone sat in dumbfounded silence. No one moved. The door to the auditorium opened and Mr. Crawford walked in with Danny Schneider, his face streaked from crying. "Danny has a few words to say," Mr. Crawford said solemnly. "I'm so sorry for all of us."

Danny moved to the front of the auditorium stage next to Coach Waters. "I was with Tyler this morning in his hospital room when he..." Danny didn't finish the sentence as he tried to regain his composure. "But after I left the hospital, I kept thinking what we could do for Tyler. We all know how much he wanted to win forty matches this season, to set the state record and be remembered for something. And then I knew what *we* had to do for him as a team." He wiped away the tears that clouded his eyes. "He was willing to give up the record to show how much he loved our coaches and what they taught us about being men. We already showed that. The coaches know how we feel about them in our hearts." He looked at his teammates and said in an almost pleading voice. "Now it's our time to show Tyler how much we loved him. Let's get Tyler that fortieth win. I say we wrestle Mecklenburg. Not for us, but for Tyler."

For a moment the auditorium was silent as everyone tried to understand what Danny was saying. Then Stevie Reynolds stood up. "For Tyler," he said simply.

We all rose in unison from our seats and said one after another, "For Tyler."

Coach Waters looked at Jimmie Ray, then at us as tears streamed down our faces. "For Tyler," he nodded.

* * * * *

On Wednesday afternoon our team stood quietly in the Mecklenburg locker room waiting to be weighed in for the match. For the first time that I could ever remember, the Mecklenburg wrestlers quietly mingled with the Harpers Ferry boys. The usual look of arrogance and social superiority that had always been their trademark was gone, replaced by a genuine showing of grief for their cross-county rivals. It was a somber setting, but one filled with a sense of unity in sorrow, of an odd togetherness.

The Mecklenburg 95-pounder stepped off the scales after weighing in. "Coach, do you have a 95-pound wrestler?" asked referee Bubba Taylor, looking at one of our wrestlers who appeared to weigh about 95 pounds.

Coach Waters looked up at the ceiling for a moment. "The 95-pound weight class is Tyler Moore's starting spot," Coach responded as his eyes dropped to the floor. "I think he's weighing in someplace else right now."

The Mecklenburg head coach nodded. Lenny Langston had resigned as an assistant coach the day before when he heard we wanted to wrestle after Tyler's death. He didn't want to be a distraction.

Bill Moore and his wife sat in the stands for the match. Although they were filled with grief as they planned Tyler's funeral on Friday, they knew Tyler would want them at the match. They also knew that Tyler would be there with them, watching the match from above. Everyone seemed to know about Tyler's death. The usual festive mood and excitement of a wrestling match was gone. There was no hurling of insults or name-calling from the Mecklenburg stands as their fans politely clapped when Harpers Ferry quickly jumped out into the lead. When it was time for the 95-pound match, no one moved. Bubba Taylor motioned to the Mecklenburg coach to send out his 95-pound wrestler who had weighed in earlier. The coach walked out on the mat to whisper to the referee. Bubba nodded.

Bubba stepped forward to face the stands and shouted, "Mecklenburg forfeits the 95-pound weight class to the memory of Tyler Moore."

The people in the bleachers exchanged confused glances until Lenny Langston stood up and quietly began clapping. Other Mecklenburg fans stood and joined in the clapping until, one by one, everyone in the gymnasium, Mecklenburg and Harpers Ferry fans alike, was standing, clapping and cheering in a crescendo of warm applause.

When Artie Badger pinned his heavyweight opponent to end the match, we had easily secured a 67-13 win. Our final record was 40-0, a new West Virginia state record. But unlike the previous weekend's tournament, there was no joyous jumping up and down and celebrating. Parents came down from the stands and gave us hugs, and there was some crying, but if there was any happiness it seemed a thousand miles away. This time the Mecklenburg wrestlers lined up to shake our hands, and when they did, the boys who had taunted Harpers Ferry and been our adversaries for two or three years gave us double-handshakes or embracing hugs.

The war was over.

43

Tyler Moore's funeral service was held on Friday afternoon at Harpers Ferry Junior High School. Word had spread quickly throughout the county about his death, and especially how the Mecklenburg wrestling coach had forfeited the 95-pound match to the memory of Tyler Moore. It had somehow brought the community together. The grief over Tyler's death was felt by everyone.

Hundreds of folding chairs had been placed on the floor of the gymnasium and the bleachers pulled out to capacity. But even before the service began, many late-arriving people were forced to stand along the walls. Snow had begun falling several hours earlier, but still the people came. It was a turnout of people from all walks of life in the county--friends and teachers, teammates and coaches, the rich, the poor, the elderly, the young, and people who simply cared.

They came from other parts of the state, too. Coach Dave Walker of Independence Junior High sat in the bleachers with his young son. Coach Sal of Braxton County was there with a large number of her players and their parents, including Dig, whose eyes were already red as he stared blankly across the gym floor at the brick walls. Even the coach from George Mason High School in Virginia was there with Kyle and several of his teammates. Kyle kept looking at the picture of Tyler that was draped behind the podium and never moved a muscle. The

Mecklenburg Junior High wrestling team arrived together, smartly dressed in white shirts and ties. Some of the boys nodded with sad, frowning faces to members of our wrestling team who had turned around to look at them.

The contingent of people sat quietly as we watched a photo journal of Tyler's life on a massive screen that had been set up at the front of the gymnasium. The public address system gently played the John Denver song, *"County Roads."* The words spilled out. *"Almost Heaven, West Virginia. Blue Ridge Mountain, Shenandoah River..."*

There were pictures of Tyler as a baby and pictures of Tyler as a little boy playing baseball and wrestling around with Big Bill. Other photos showed Tyler riding a horse on his grandparents' farm and in another he was pretending to be Paul Bunyon as he held an ax in one hand. His foot rested on a pile of split firewood as he proudly flexed his muscles. There were photos of him and Danny goofing around together through the years as they aged in front of everyone's eyes. Another showed him accepting his first championship trophy in wrestling. There was one constant in all the photos. Tyler was always smiling. Always happy. You'd think he was just a normal kid.

The last picture to be shown was the team photo that had been taken only two weeks earlier. It was just the way Tyler had wanted it. Across the bottom of the picture was a handsome inscription reading:

Harpers Ferry Wrestling
1999-2000
West Virginia State Record, 40-0

Tyler was sitting in the front row, third from the right, a huge smile on his face. Travis was there next to Tyler. And up in the third row, wearing a collared shirt over an undershirt, was Tyler's best friend, Danny. We were all there.

As the pictures came to an end, the final words from Tyler's favorite song echoed from the speakers above the audience. *"Take me home, down country roads."* Many of the people in the crowd put their heads down and bit their lips.

Danny then got up and tried his best to talk about Tyler, but it was too much for him. About the only words that Danny managed to say coherently was, "The last thing Tyler told me was that he just wanted to be a normal kid." Then he broke down, too choked up to continue.

The people in the audience shifted nervously, waiting for Coach Waters to get up and say something. We all knew he would. Finally he went to the podium. This was far tougher than any wrestling match he had ever coached, and he made sure he was very composed. So with a smile on his face, he told the people about Tyler's first year of wrestling at Harpers Ferry. How his only win was the last match of the season that ended with him leaping deliriously through the air into the arms of his father, who swung him around the mat in victory as the crowd went wild. Everyone laughed.

Then Coach Waters grew serious and went on to explain how Tyler had never given up in *anything,* how he always strived to be a better person and led the team by example. "When I first learned that Tyler had died, I went back and looked up his record. He won thirty-one matches this year, well, thirty-two," he smiled, nodding to the Mecklenburg team. "Tyler was the most selfless person I ever knew. He had a charisma about him that drew people to him and brought people together. Call it his *Mountain Magic.* He always knew that unless a miracle happened, he was probably doomed to an early death." Coach paused and inhaled a deep breath. "Imagine having to live with that thought every day of your life like Tyler did. But he never complained. He never used his illness as a crutch. All Tyler ever wanted to be was a normal kid. Just like anyone else. But perhaps that was the only thing in Tyler's life that he failed at. You see, Tyler Moore was not a normal boy. Instead, he was an extraordinary person, with more guts and courage than me or you or anyone else I know. He was truly a one-of-a-kind young man."

When the service was over, people filed quietly out of the gymnasium. The snow was coming down harder. But as the long procession of cars and trucks made its way through the snow to the cemetery, not a single vehicle broke line.

Epilogue

Today, at the entrance to Harpers Ferry, there is a sign that commemorates a single achievement that brought a small community together. It reads, exactly:

HARPERS FERRY
HOME OF THE WEST VIRGINIA
STATE RECORD
WRESTLING TEAM
40-0
1999-2000

Tyler Moore hasn't stopped smiling.

Where Are They Now?

Tunction
This book is a work of fiction, with many names, places, and events being the product of my imagination. However, Tyler Moore is a very real person, and so are many of the Harpers Ferry wrestlers. After all, they were friends and teammates. I thought it would be interesting to say a few things about the boys whose real names were used in this book (with their permission), such as what they're doing now and where they live. (Facebook is an amazing resource for finding people!)

Unfortunately, I wasn't able to track everyone down, but I was able to get in touch with many of the boys. They really haven't changed much. They're still so polite and respectful, and truly the greatest bunch of kids that I've ever coached. Funny, even though it's been more than ten years, I still think of them as being fourteen or fifteen. Still kids. And it seems like only yesterday that Tyler was running wind sprints through the upstairs hallway at Harpers Ferry, getting in shape with the rest of his friends, promising them a dream if they'd only believe in themselves.

Here's what some of the boys are doing today:

Chris *"The Little Beast"* Galford: Chris says he misses the care-free days of goofing around and wrestling at Harpers Ferry, and especially seeing his old teammates. The Beast hasn't changed much. He still calls Harpers Ferry home.

Ronnie Dillow: Ronnie graduated from West Virginia University and works at Hollywood Casino at Charles Town. He lives in nearby Berkeley County.

Stevie Reynolds: Stevie finally did get his undefeated season in wrestling. As a senior in high school, he marched through the season with an undefeated record that culminated with him winning the West Virginia state championship. He went on to Lehigh University, earning his degree in Civil Engineering. He now lives in Frederick, Maryland, and works as a lead design engineer for his firm.

Travis Nutter: Travis lives with his wife and three children in the Beckley, West Virginia area. Ten years after leaving Harpers Ferry, teammate Mike "Smitty" Smith would show him what true friendship is all about. Travis works today as a proud West Virginia coal miner.

Danny Schneider: Danny has always had a love of horses and works at the Charles Town Race Track and lives in Charles Town. He thinks of Tyler every day.

Evan Whalen: Evan is attending Shepherd University, located in Shepherdstown, West Virginia. He plans on going to graduate school after getting his undergraduate degree. He still lives in the Harpers Ferry area.

Doug "Psycho" Sillex: Doug works for Marriott International where he manages data and telecom installs for their data center. He lives in nearby Hagerstown, Maryland.

Mike "Smitty" Smith: Mike has served his country by taking a tour of duty in Iraq and is awaiting his next deployment. In 2010, when Travis Nutter's house burned to the ground, Mike and several other wrestlers left the same day for the six-hour drive to Beckley, West Virginia, to help Travis pick up the pieces of his life. They were still a team.

Artie Badger: Artie is presently attending Concord University and working toward his degree in Education with an emphasis in music. When he graduates from college, Artie would like to coach wrestling at a local high school in the county. He still lives in Harpers Ferry.

Coach Roland Proctor: Roland attended Shepherd University and lives on Blue Ridge Mountain.

Coach Bill Moore: Big Bill recently built a new house and lives on a farm in Maysville, Grant County, West Virginia.

Coach Jimmie Ray Lawson: Jim has been the vocational teacher at Harpers Ferry Junior High/Middle School for twenty-four years and is still going strong. He continues to be the most popular teacher at Harpers Ferry.

Coach Mac Waters: Mac Waters, a.k.a. Malcolm Ater, is the author of this novel.

Special Thanks

I would like to thank the following people for their tremendous help and encouragement in assisting me through the various stages of writing and editing this novel.

Lauren Carr: Lauren provided me with invaluable assistance in writing this novel, in all areas, and also handled the layout for the inside of the book. She has penned four murder mysteries, with her latest novel, *Old Loves Die Hard,* due out in May, 2011.

Bob O'Connor: Bob gave me hope and encouragement in his publishing class, and also proofread my story for mistakes. He has authored six Civil War era historical fiction novels, the most recent being *The Life of Abraham Lincoln as President.*

Adel Knott: When it comes to a crackerjack proofreader, Adel is at the top of the class. The media-center specialist at Harpers Ferry has painstakingly gone over my writings and always has nice things to say, regardless of how many errors she finds.

Jared Sheerer: Jared handled the design and layout for the front and back cover with uncompromising success.

Jason Hoffman and Nick Kosanovich: Many thanks for the excellent photographs on the cover of this novel, and for their patience in getting the "perfect shots."

And finally, very special thanks to my best friend and mentor, Clarence "Bones" Wright, who listened to my hopes and dreams about writing for twenty-seven years. He picked me up so many times when I was ready to quit, especially during the difficult times of writing *Tyler's Mountain Magic,* and without his prodding and encouragement this book would never have been finished. I wish he was here to read it.

About the Author

Malcolm Ater has been the special education reading teacher at Harpers Ferry Junior High and Harpers Ferry Middle School for twenty-three years. He is most proud of the fact that between 2005 and 2009, his students had the highest combined special education reading achievement test scores of any middle school in West Virginia during that four-year period.

He was also the assistant wrestling coach under the guidance of head coach Jimmie Ray Lawson for five years at Harpers Ferry Junior High and the head coach from 1997 to 2001. He was the fastest coach in West Virginia secondary school history to win 100 career games or matches. His four-year record as a head coach was 110 wins and 14 losses.

Over the years, he has frequently contributed human interest stories to *Goldenseal,* the official state magazine of West Virginia. Malcolm has also written three educational sixteen-page comic books, two for The American Cancer Society, *Taking a Chance...With No Chance to Win,* and *So You Want to Stop? You Can!* His other educational comic was for the Centers for Disease Control and endorsed by the U.S. Surgeon General, *What You Know About AIDS Can Save Your Life.* All three comics reached distribution levels of well over a million copies each.

Malcolm earned his B.S. in Education from Old Dominion University where he was a varsity baseball pitcher. He earned his master's degree in Special Education from West Virginia University.

For ordering additional books or speaking engagements, Malcolm can be contacted at (304) 876-6985 or through either of his email addresses:

player3519@hotmail.com

BlueRidgeMountainBooks@hotmail.com